The Return of
The Mucker

The Return of
The Mucker

Edgar Rice Burroughs

WILDSIDE PRESS
Doylestown, Pennsylvania

The Return of the Mucker
A publication of
WILDSIDE PRESS
P.O. Box 301
Holicong, PA 18928-0301

www.wildsidepress.com

INTRODUCTION:

Master of Our Imagination

*I*f there is such a thing as a "collective subconscious" as proposed by Jung, then Edgar Rice Burroughs leapt into it and never left in 1917 when *Tarzan of the Apes* was published in England, and Burroughs's first Mars book found readers. That was the year before the end of the "Great War," a year of great trouble, and the aftermath of the terrible Influenza epidemic. Millions died in Europe and around the world, soldiers within the trenches, and civilians due to disease, starvation, and economic upheaval.

Imagine the Lord of Greystoke, raised in the Jungle. A man of honor, courage, and uncompromising principles, who knew nothing of Continental politics, Bolshevism, or anarchists with knives, guns and bombs. Imagine, too, a Mars of wonder, with great lords, Princesses, barbarians, and wondrous new inventions. And imagine them coming into a world of trouble and strife. Dreams do serve a purpose; and Edgar Rice Burroughs was nothing if not a great and powerful dreamer.

Burroughs's aficionados note that during his life-time, his work "failed to gather critical acclaim, yet influenced a generation." Like so many beloved writers, Burroughs followed the well-known path to storytelling success. Burroughs got a start in writing after some failed attempts at being a salesman, railroad policeman, and other professions; according to official biographies, he even had to pawn his wife's jewelry to make ends meet. He daydreamed and read pulp magazines, and one day decided that he could write a better pulp story than the ones he knew, and submitted his first tale to the *All-Story Magazine* at age 35, using the pseudonym "Normal Bean," believing that the story was so far-out and fantastic that no one would be interested. He shouldn't have worried. From that time forward, readers were hooked.

What can you say about a writer who created Tarzan of the Apes, John Carter of Mars, and David Innes of Pellucidar? A writer who took readers — for the first time, and for many, the times that they imagine and dream and remember always — to the African jungles, to the plains and canals of Mars, and to the magical world of Pellucidar? Worlds within our own, far more wondrous than any ever imagined before — Barsoom! Ray Bradbury fully acknowledges his debt to Edgar Rice Burroughs, and in this beautiful, childlike, dreaming bard's words can we see the reflection of Burroughs's dreams today. In truth, nearly every fantasy or science fiction writer, and certainly filmmakers, have drunk from the well of Edgar Rice Burroughs, and drunk deeply.

Ray Bradbury never spoke more movingly than at the Nebula Awards in 2001 in Beverly Hills, California. There is something of magic in him, just as there is something of complete wonder and magic in Edgar

Rice Burroughs. Ray Bradbury spoke, as he often does, of the importance of remaining a child, and this is true: there is something of the child in almost every great writer. Do you remember when you were young? How it seemed that if you only wished hard enough and thought hard enough and dreamed long enough, the magic might become real? Toys were not merely playthings, they were real, real friends, real companions, real comrades. And that boy in the jungle that every child knows, swinging from the trees, he can really talk to the lions and the elephants and the crocodiles and to "Cheetah." Tarzan can even talk to Jane. Now, if that's not magic, what is?

No one much compliments Burroughs on his prose, but here is how he introduces John Carter in *A Princess of Mars*: "I am a very old man; how old I do not know. Possibly I am a hundred, possibly more; but I cannot tell because I have never aged as other men, nor do I remember any childhood. So far as I can recollect I have always been a man, a man of about thirty. I appear today as I did forty years and more ago, and yet I feel that I cannot go on living forever; that some day I shall die the real death from which there is no resurrection." Perhaps the suggestion of Carter's agelessness is what offends "critics," but — John Carter may have feared that he would die the "real death," but the truth is — he'll live forever.

Chieftains, Princesses, Adventurers, Barbarians. Lush jungles, garden worlds, and a world within the Earth itself. This is the imagination of a profound dreamer, full of rich images that have fueled more than fifty Tarzan movies and famous Tarzans from Johnny Weismuller and Buster Crabbe to Ron Ely and Christopher Lambert. Fritz Leiber and Philip Jose Farmer have written Tarzan-inspired novels. It doesn't matter how many NASA probes return from Mars empty-handed: dreamers everywhere know that somewhere, sometime, somehow, Barsoom is real.

At the very Nebula Award ceremony where Ray Bradbury spoke, Philip Jose Farmer was named one of science fiction's "Grand Masters." Farmer came up with the idea that there is some kind of vast genetic "family" of heroes and adventurers, all related, and among these are Tarzan, John Carter, and other beloved Burroughs characters. This all sounds quite insane, but how else to explain this extraordinary combination of heroism, strength, and character?

Just like 1917, we are in a world whose moorings have come loose, a world filled with change, fear, and horrific, cataclysmic events. Perhaps these stories of Edgar Rice Burroughs, filled with wonder, adventure, miracles, heroes and villains as they are, fit the same need today as they did during that long-ago time. A distant jungle, to ponder about and imagine, a hero swinging to the rescue, calling nature itself to his aid. A man of adventure, beyond age and limitations, traversing the magical, mystical land of Mars. Pellucidar, whose very name conjures up images of beauty, mystery and wonder.

We are told that to grow up, we must put aside childish things; but what child ever went to war? What child ever flew a plane into a building which was itself a miracle, killing thousands, like the World Trade Towers? And who was ever too old to breathe in wonder at untold vistas beneath the earth, to think that a Princess of Mars was beautiful, to imagine the gardens of Mars and the deep, green jungles of Africa where a man grew to be a hero untouched by human hand?

Edgar Rice Burroughs himself told everyone that his only aim in writing was to "entertain." He wanted to take people's minds off their troubles for a few moments, give them laughter, pleasure and enjoyment.

Few, if any, have ever so entertained. Not just one, but many of his characters are as real to us as if they truly lived, breathed and walked. They are truly immortal: Tarzan will never die; John Carter still lives.

There is too much pain in this world, and too little wonder. Every so often, we receive gifts. And these, like Edgar Rice Burroughs, we ought not question, but rather, treasure.

Edgar Rice Burroughs created a full, rich panoply of characters and worlds of wonder. His work is timeless, like one of his invented worlds: *The Land That Time Forgot*. Edgar Rice Burroughs made pure, unadulterated magic.

— Amy Sterling Casil
February, 2002
Redlands, California

Chapter I

THE MURDER TRIAL

*B*illy Byrne squared his broad shoulders and filled his deep lungs with the familiar medium which is known as air in Chicago. He was standing upon the platform of a New York Central train that was pulling into the La Salle Street Station, and though the young man was far from happy something in the nature of content pervaded his being, for he was coming home.

After something more than a year of world wandering and strange adventure Billy Byrne was coming back to the great West Side and Grand Avenue.

Now there is not much upon either side or down the center of long and tortuous Grand Avenue to arouse enthusiasm, nor was Billy particularly enthusiastic about that more or less squalid thoroughfare.

The thing that exalted Billy was the idea that he was coming back to *show them*. He had left under a cloud and with a reputation for genuine toughness and rowdyism that has seen few parallels even in the ungentle district of his birth and upbringing.

A girl had changed him. She was as far removed from Billy's sphere as the stars themselves; but Billy had loved her and learned from her, and in trying to become more as he knew the men of her class were he had sloughed off much of the uncouthness that had always been a part of him, and all of the rowdyism. Billy Byrne was no longer the mucker.

He had given her up because he imagined the gulf between Grand Avenue and Riverside Drive to be unbridgeable; but he still clung to the ideals she had awakened in him. He still sought to be all that she might wish him to be, even though he realized that he never should see her again.

Grand Avenue would be the easiest place to forget his sorrow — her he could never forget. And then, his newly awakened pride urged him back to the haunts of his former life that he might, as he would put it himself, show them. He wanted the gang to see that he, Billy Byrne, wasn't afraid to be decent. He wanted some of the neighbors to realize that he could work steadily and earn an honest living, and he looked forward with delight to the pleasure and satisfaction of rubbing it in to some of the saloon keepers and bartenders who had helped keep him drunk some five days out of seven, for Billy didn't drink any more.

But most of all he wanted to vindicate himself in the eyes of the once-hated law. He wanted to clear his record of the unjust charge of murder which had sent him scurrying out of Chicago over a year before, that night that Patrolman Stanley Lasky of the Lake Street Station had tipped him off that Sheehan had implicated him in the murder of old man Schneider.

Now Billy Byrne had not killed Schneider. He had been nowhere near the old fellow's saloon at the time of the holdup; but Sheehan, who had been arrested and charged with the crime, was an old enemy of Billy's, and Sheehan had seen a chance to divert some of the suspicion from himself and square accounts with Byrne at the same time.

The new Billy Byrne was ready to accept at face value everything which seemed to belong in any way to the environment of that exalted realm where dwelt the girl he loved. Law, order, and justice appeared to Billy in a new light since he had rubbed elbows with the cultured and refined.

He no longer distrusted or feared them. They would give him what he sought — a square deal.

It seemed odd to Billy that he should be seeking anything from the law or its minions. For years he had waged a perpetual battle with both. Now he was coming back voluntarily to give himself up, with every conviction that he should be exonerated quickly. Billy, knowing his own innocence, realizing his own integrity, assumed that others must immediately appreciate both.

"First," thought Billy, "I'll go take a look at little old Grand Ave., then I'll give myself up. The trial may take a long time, an' if it does I want to see some of the old bunch first."

So Billy entered an "L" coach and leaning on the sill of an open window watched grimy Chicago rattle past until the guard's "Granavenoo" announced the end of his journey.

Maggie Shane was sitting on the upper step of the long flight of stairs which lean precariously against the scarred face of the frame residence upon the second floor front of which the lares and penates of the Shane family are crowded into three ill-smelling rooms.

It was Saturday and Maggie was off. She sat there rather disconsolate for there was a dearth of beaux for Maggie, none having arisen to fill the aching void left by the sudden departure of "Coke" Sheehan since that

worthy gentleman had sought a more salubrious clime
— to the consternation of both Maggie Shane and Mr.
Sheehan's bondsmen.

Maggie scowled down upon the frowsy street filled
with frowsy women and frowsy children. She scowled
upon the street cars rumbling by with their frowsy
loads. Occasionally she varied the monotony by draw-
ing out her chewing gum to wondrous lengths, holding
one end between a thumb and finger and the other
between her teeth.

Presently Maggie spied a rather pleasing figure saun-
tering up the sidewalk upon her side of the street. The
man was too far away for her to recognize his features,
but his size and bearing and general appearance appealed to the lonesome Maggie. She hoped it was
someone she knew, or with whom she might easily
become acquainted, for Maggie was bored to death.

She patted the hair at the back of her head and
righted the mop which hung over one eye. Then she
rearranged her skirts and waited. As the man approached she saw that he was better looking than she
had even dared to hope, and that there was something
extremely familiar about his appearance. It was not,
though, until he was almost in front of the house that
he looked up at the girl and she recognized him.

Then Maggie Shane gasped and clutched the hand-
rail at her side. An instant later the man was past and
continuing his way along the sidewalk.

Maggie Shane glared after him for a minute, then
she ran quickly down the stairs and into a grocery store
a few doors west, where she asked if she might use the
telephone.

"Gimme West 2063," she demanded of the operator,
and a moment later: "Is this Lake Street?"

"Well say, Billy Byrne's back. I just see him."

"Yes an' never mind who I am; but if youse guys want

him he's walkin' west on Grand Avenoo right now. I just this minute seen him near Lincoln," and she smashed the receiver back into its hook.

Billy Byrne thought that he would look in on his mother, not that he expected to be welcomed even though she might happen to be sober, or not that he cared to see her; but Billy's whole manner of thought had altered within the year, and something now seemed to tell him that it was his duty to do the thing he contemplated. Maybe he might even be of help to her.

But when he reached the gloomy neighborhood in which his childhood had been spent it was to learn that his mother was dead and that another family occupied the tumble-down cottage that had been his home.

If Billy Byrne felt any sorrow because of his mother's death he did not reveal it outwardly. He owed her nothing but for kicks and cuffs received, and for the surroundings and influences that had started him upon a life of crime at an age when most boys are just entering grammar school.

Really the man was relieved that he had not had to see her, and it was with a lighter step that he turned back to retrace his way along Grand Avenue. No one of the few he had met who recognized him had seemed particularly delighted at his return. The whole affair had been something of a disappointment. Therefore Billy determined to go at once to the Lake Street Station and learn the status of the Schneider murder case. Possibly they had discovered the real murderer, and if that was the case Billy would be permitted to go his way; but if not then he could give himself up and ask for a trial, that he might be exonerated.

As he neared Wood Street two men who had been watching his approach stepped into the doorway of a saloon, and as he passed they stepped out again behind him. One upon either side they seized him.

Billy turned to remonstrate.

"Come easy now, Byrne," admonished one of the men, "an' don't make no fuss."

"Oh," said Billy, "it's you, is it? Well, I was just goin' over to the station to give myself up."

Both men laughed, skeptically. "We'll just save you the trouble," said one of them. "We'll take you over. You might lose your way if you tried to go alone."

Billy went along in silence the rest of the way to where the patrol waited at another corner. He saw there was nothing to be gained by talking to these detectives; but he found the lieutenant equally inclined to doubt his intentions. He, too, only laughed when Billy assured him that he was on his way to the station at the very instant of arrest.

As the weeks dragged along, and Billy Byrne found no friendly interest in himself or his desire to live on the square, and no belief in his protestations that he had had naught to do with the killing of Schneider he began to have his doubts as to the wisdom of his act.

He also commenced to entertain some of his former opinions of the police, and of the law of which they are supposed to be the guardians. A cell-mate told him that the papers had scored the department heavily for their failure to apprehend the murderer of the inoffensive old Schneider, and that public opinion had been so aroused that a general police shakeup had followed.

The result was that the police were keen to fasten the guilt upon someone — they did not care whom, so long as it was someone who was in their custody.

"You may not o' done it," ventured the cell-mate; "but they'll send you up for it, if they can't hang you. They're goin' to try to get the death sentence. They hain't got no love for you, Byrne. You caused 'em a lot o' throuble in your day an' they haven't forgot it. I'd hate to be in your boots."

Billy Byrne shrugged. Where were his dreams of justice? They seemed to have faded back into the old distrust and hatred. He shook himself and conjured in his mind the vision of a beautiful girl who had believed in him and trusted him — who had inculcated within him a love for all that was finest and best in true manhood, for the very things that he had most hated all the years of his life before she had come into his existence to alter it and him.

And then Billy would believe again — believe that in the end justice would triumph and that it would all come out right, just the way he had pictured it.

With the coming of the last day of the trial Billy found it more and more difficult to adhere to his regard for law, order, and justice. The prosecution had shown conclusively that Billy was a hard customer. The police had brought witnesses who did not hesitate to perjure themselves in their testimony — testimony which it seemed to Billy the densest of jurymen could plainly see had been framed up and learned by rote until it was letter-perfect.

These witnesses could recall with startling accuracy every detail that had occurred between seventeen minutes after eight and twenty-one minutes past nine on the night of September 23 over a year before; but where they had been and what they had done ten minutes earlier or ten minutes later, or where they were at nine o'clock in the evening last Friday they couldn't for the lives of them remember.

And Billy was practically without witnesses.

The result was a foregone conclusion. Even Billy had to admit it, and when the prosecuting attorney demanded the death penalty the prisoner had an uncanny sensation as of the tightening of a hempen rope about his neck.

As he waited for the jury to return its verdict Billy sat in his cell trying to read a newspaper which a kindly guard had given him. But his eyes persisted in boring through the white paper and the black type to scenes that were not in any paper. He saw a turbulent river tumbling through a savage world, and in the swirl of the water lay a little island. And he saw a man there upon the island, and a girl. The girl was teaching the man to speak the language of the cultured, and to view life as people of refinement view it.

She taught him what honor meant among her class, and that it was better to lose any other possession rather than lose honor. Billy realized that it had been these lessons that had spurred him on to the mad scheme that was to end now with the verdict of "Guilty" — he had wished to vindicate his honor. A hard laugh broke from his lips; but instantly he sobered and his face softened.

It had been for her sake after all, and what mattered it if they did send him to the gallows? He had not sacrificed his honor — he had done his best to assert it. He was innocent. They could kill him but they couldn't make him guilty. A thousand juries pronouncing him so could not make it true that he had killed Schneider.

But it would be hard, after all his hopes, after all the plans he had made to live square, to *show them*. His eyes still boring through the paper suddenly found themselves attracted by something in the text before them — a name, Harding.

Billy Byrne shook himself and commenced to read:

The marriage of Barbara, daughter of Anthony Harding, the multimillionaire, to William Mallory will take place on the twenty-fifth of June.

The article was dated New York. There was more, but Billy did not read it. He had read enough. It is true that he had urged her to marry Mallory; but now, in his lonesomeness and friendlessness, he felt almost as though she had been untrue to him.

"Come along, Byrne," a bailiff interrupted his thoughts, "the jury's reached a verdict."

The judge was emerging from his chambers as Billy was led into the courtroom. Presently the jury filed in and took their seats. The foreman handed the clerk a bit of paper. Even before it was read Billy knew that he had been found guilty. He did not care any longer, so he told himself. He hoped that the judge would send him to the gallows. There was nothing more in life for him now anyway. He wanted to die. But instead he was sentenced to life imprisonment in the penitentiary at Joliet.

This was infinitely worse than death. Billy Byrne was appalled at the thought of remaining for life within the grim stone walls of a prison. Once more there swept over him all the old, unreasoning hatred of the law and all that pertained to it. He would like to close his steel fingers about the fat neck of the red-faced judge. The smug jurymen roused within him the lust to kill. Justice! Billy Byrne laughed aloud.

A bailiff rapped for order. One of the jurymen leaned close to a neighbor and whispered. "A hardened criminal," he said. "Society will be safer when he is behind the bars."

The next day they took Billy aboard a train bound for Joliet. He was handcuffed to a deputy sheriff. Billy was calm outwardly; but inwardly he was a raging volcano of hate.

*I*n a certain very beautiful home on Riverside Drive, New York City, a young lady, comfortably backed by downy pillows, sat in her bed and alternated her attention between coffee and rolls, and a morning paper.

On the inside of the main sheet a heading claimed her languid attention: Chicago Murderer Given Life Sentence. Of late Chicago had aroused in Barbara Harding a greater proportion of interest than ever it had in the past, and so it was that she now permitted her eyes to wander casually down the printed column.

Murderer of harmless old saloon keeper is finally brought to justice. The notorious West Side rowdy, "Billy" Byrne, apprehended after more than a year as fugitive from justice, is sent to Joliet for life.

Barbara Harding sat stony-eyed and cold for what seemed many minutes. Then with a stifled sob she turned and buried her face in the pillows.

The train bearing Billy Byrne and the deputy sheriff toward Joliet had covered perhaps half the distance between Chicago and Billy's permanent destination when it occurred to the deputy sheriff that he should like to go into the smoker and enjoy a cigar.

Now, from the moment that he had been sentenced Billy Byrne's mind had been centered upon one thought — escape. He knew that there probably would be not the slightest chance for escape; but nevertheless the idea was always uppermost in his thoughts.

His whole being revolted, not alone against the injustice which had sent him into life imprisonment, but at the thought of the long years of awful monotony which lay ahead of him.

He could not endure them. He would not! The

deputy sheriff rose, and motioning his prisoner ahead of him, started for the smoker. It was two cars ahead. The train was vestibuled. The first platform they crossed was tightly enclosed; but at the second Billy saw that a careless porter had left one of the doors open. The train was slowing down for some reason — it was going, perhaps, twenty miles an hour.

Billy was the first upon the platform. He was the first to see the open door. It meant one of two things — a chance to escape, or, death. Even the latter was to be preferred to life imprisonment.

Billy did not hesitate an instant. Even before the deputy sheriff realized that the door was open, his prisoner had leaped from the moving train dragging his guard after him.

Chapter II

THE ESCAPE

*B*yrne had no time to pick any particular spot to jump for. When he did jump he might have been directly over a picket fence, or a bottomless pit — he did not know. Nor did he care.

As it happened he was over neither. The platform chanced to be passing across a culvert at the instant. Beneath the culvert was a slimy pool. Into this the two men plunged, alighting unharmed.

Byrne was the first to regain his feet. He dragged the deputy sheriff to his knees, and before that frightened and astonished officer of the law could gather his wits together he had been relieved of his revolver and found himself looking into its cold and business-like muzzle.

Then Billy Byrne waded ashore, prodding the deputy sheriff in the ribs with cold steel, and warning him to silence. Above the pool stood a little wood, thick with tangled wildwood. Into this Byrne forced his prisoner.

When they had come deep enough into the concealment of the foliage to make discovery from the outside improbable Byrne halted.

"Now say yer prayers," he commanded. "I'm a-going to croak yeh."

The deputy sheriff looked up at him in wild-eyed terror.

"My God!" he cried. "I ain't done nothin' to you, Byrne. Haven't I always been your friend? What've I ever done to you? For God's sake Byrne you ain't goin' to murder me, are you? They'll get you, sure."

Billy Byrne let a rather unpleasant smile curl his lips.

"No," he said, "youse ain't done nothin' to me; but you stand for the law, damn it, and I'm going to croak everything I meet that stands for the law. They wanted to send me up for life — me, an innocent man. Your kind done it — the cops. You ain't no cop; but you're just as rotten. Now say yer prayers."

He leveled the revolver at his victim's head. The deputy sheriff slumped to his knees and tried to embrace Billy Byrne's legs as he pleaded for his life.

"Cut it out, you poor boob," admonished Billy. "You've gotta die and if you was half a man you'd wanna die like one."

The deputy sheriff slipped to the ground. His terror had overcome him, leaving him in happy unconsciousness. Byrne stood looking down upon the man for a moment. His wrist was chained to that of the other, and the pull of the deputy's body was irritating.

Byrne stooped and placed the muzzle of the revolver back of the man's ear. "Justice!" he muttered, scornfully, and his finger tightened upon the trigger.

Then, conjured from nothing, there rose between himself and the unconscious man beside him the figure of a beautiful girl. Her face was brave and smiling, and in her eyes was trust and pride — whole worlds of them. Trust and pride in Billy Byrne.

Billy closed his eyes tight as though in physical pain.

He brushed his hand quickly across his fare.

"Gawd!" he muttered. "I can't do it — but I came awful close to it."

Dropping the revolver into his side pocket he kneeled beside the deputy sheriff and commenced to go through the man's clothes. After a moment he came upon what he sought — a key ring confining several keys.

Billy found the one he wished and presently he was free. He still stood looking at the deputy sheriff.

"I ought to croak you," he murmured. "I'll never make my get-away if I don't; but *she* won't let me — God bless her."

Suddenly a thought came to Billy Byrne. If he could have a start he might escape. It wouldn't hurt the man any to stay here for a few hours, or even for a day. Billy removed the deputy's coat and tore it into strips. With these he bound the man to a tree. Then he fastened a gag in his mouth.

During the operation the deputy regained consciousness. He looked questioningly at Billy.

"I decided not to croak you," explained the young man. "I'm just a-goin' to leave you here for a while. They'll be lookin' all along the right o' way in a few hours — it won't be long afore they find you. Now so long, and take care of yerself, bo," and Billy Byrne had gone.

A mistake that proved fortunate for Billy Byrne caused the penitentiary authorities to expect him and his guard by a later train, so no suspicion was aroused when they failed to come upon the train they really had started upon. This gave Billy a good two hours' start that he would not otherwise have had — an opportunity of which he made good use.

Wherefore it was that by the time the authorities awoke to the fact that something had happened Billy

Byrne was fifty miles west of Joliet, bowling along aboard a fast Santa Fe freight. Shortly after night had fallen the train crossed the Mississippi. Billy Byrne was hungry and thirsty, and as the train slowed down and came to a stop out in the midst of a dark solitude of silent, sweet-smelling country, Billy opened the door of his box car and dropped lightly to the ground.

So far no one had seen Billy since he had passed from the ken of the trussed deputy sheriff, and as Billy had no desire to be seen he slipped over the edge of the embankment into a dry ditch, where he squatted upon his haunches waiting for the train to depart. The stop out there in the dark night was one of those mysterious stops which trains are prone to make, un-explained and doubtless unexplainable by any other than a higher intelligence which directs the movements of men and rolling stock. There was no town, and not even a switch light. Presently two staccato blasts broke from the engine's whistle, there was a progressive jerk-ing at coupling pins, which started up at the big locomotive and ran rapidly down the length of the train, there was the squeaking of brake shoes against wheels, and the train moved slowly forward again upon its long journey toward the coast, gaining momentum moment by moment until finally the way-car rolled rapidly past the hidden fugitive and the freight rum-bled away to be swallowed up in the darkness.

When it had gone Billy rose and climbed back upon the track, along which he plodded in the wake of the departing train. Somewhere a road would presently cut across the track, and along the road there would be farmhouses or a village where food and drink might be found.

Billy was penniless, yet he had no doubt but that he should eat when he had discovered food. He was think-ing of this as he walked briskly toward the west, and what he thought of induced a doubt in his mind as to whether it was, after all, going to be so easy to steal food.

"Shaw!" he exclaimed, half aloud, "she wouldn't think it wrong for a guy to swipe a little grub when he was starvin'. It ain't like I was goin' to stick a guy up for his roll. Sure she wouldn't see nothin' wrong for me to get something to eat. I ain't got no money. They took it all away from me, an' I got a right to live — but, somehow, I hate to do it. I wisht there was some other way. Gee, but she's made a sissy out o' me! Funny how a feller can change. Why I almost like bein' a sissy," and Billy Byrne grinned at the almost inconceivable idea.

Before Billy came to a road he saw a light down in a little depression at one side of the track. It was not such a light as a lamp shining beyond a window makes. It rose and fell, winking and flaring close to the ground.

It looked much like a camp fire, and as Billy drew nearer he saw that such it was, and he heard a voice, too. Billy approached more carefully. He must be careful always to see before being seen. The little fire burned upon the bank of a stream which the track bridged upon a concrete arch.

Billy dropped once more from the right of way, and climbed a fence into a thin wood. Through this he approached the camp fire with small chance of being observed. As he neared it the voice resolved itself into articulate words, and presently Billy leaned against a tree close behind the speaker and listened.

There was but a single figure beside the small fire — that of a man squatting upon his haunches roasting something above the flames. At one edge of the fire was an empty tin can from which steam arose, and an aroma that was now and again wafted to Billy's nostrils.

Coffee! My, how good it smelled. Billy's mouth

watered. But the voice — that interested Billy almost as much as the preparations for the coming meal.

We'll dance a merry saraband from here to drowsy
    Samarkand.
  Along the sea, across the land, the birds are flying
    South,
And you, my sweet Penelope, out there somewhere
    you wait for me,
  With buds, of roses in your hair and kisses on
    your mouth.

The words took hold of Billy somewhere and made him forget his hunger. Like a sweet incense which induces pleasant daydreams they were wafted in upon him through the rich, mellow voice of the solitary camper, and the lilt of the meter entered his blood.

But the voice. It was the voice of such as Billy Byrne always had loathed and ridiculed until he had sat at the feet of Barbara Harding and learned many things, including love. It was the voice of culture and refinement. Billy strained his eyes through the darkness to have a closer look at the man. The light of the camp fire fell upon frayed and bagging clothes, and upon the back of a head covered by a shapeless, and disreputable soft hat.

Obviously the man was a hobo. The coffee boiling in a discarded tin can would have been proof positive of this without other evidence; but there seemed plenty more. Yes, the man was a hobo. Billy continued to stand listening.

The mountains are all hid in mist, the valley is like
    amethyst,
The poplar leaves they turn and twist, oh, silver, sil-
    ver green!

Out there somewhere along the sea a ship is waiting
        patiently,
While up the beach the bubbles slip with white
        afloat between.

"Gee!" thought Billy Byrne; "but that's great stuff. I
wonder where he gets it. It makes me want to hike until
I find that place he's singin' about."

Billy's thoughts were interrupted by a sound in the
wood to one side of him. As he turned his eyes in the
direction of the slight noise which had attracted him
he saw two men step quietly out and cross toward the
man at the camp fire.

These, too, were evidently hobos. Doubtless pals of
the poetical one. The latter did not hear them until
they were directly behind him. Then he turned slowly
and rose as they halted beside his fire.

"Evenin', bo," said one of the newcomers.

"Good evening, gentlemen," replied the camper,
"welcome to my humble home. Have you dined?"

"Naw," replied the first speaker, "we ain't; but we're
goin' to. Now can the chatter an' duck. There ain't
enough fer one here, let alone three. Beat it!" and the
man, who was big and burly, assumed a menacing
attitude and took a truculent step nearer the solitary
camper.

The latter was short and slender. The larger man
looked as though he might have eaten him at a single
mouthful; but the camper did not flinch.

"You pain me," he said. "You induce within me a
severe and highly localized pain, and furthermore I
don't like your whiskers."

With which apparently irrelevant remark he seized
the matted beard of the larger tramp and struck the
fellow a quick, sharp blow in the face. Instantly the
fellow's companion was upon him; but the camper

retained his death grip upon the beard of the now yelling bully and continued to rain blow after blow upon head and face.

Billy Byrne was an interested spectator. He enjoyed a good fight as he enjoyed little else; but presently when the first tramp succeeded in tangling his legs about the legs of his chastiser and dragging him to the ground, and the second tramp seized a heavy stick and ran forward to dash the man's brains out, Billy thought it time to interfere.

Stepping forward he called aloud as he came: "Cut it out, boes! You can't pull off any rough stuff like that with this here sweet singer. Can it! Can it!" as the second tramp raised his stick to strike the now prostrate camper.

As he spoke Billy Byrne broke into a run, and as the stick fell he reached the man's side and swung a blow to the tramp's jaw that sent the fellow spinning backward to the river's brim, where he tottered drunkenly for a moment and then plunged backward into the shallow water.

Then Billy seized the other attacker by the shoulder and dragged him to his feet.

"Do you want some, too, you big stiff?" he inquired.

The man spluttered and tried to break away, striking at Billy as he did so; but a sudden punch, such a punch as Billy Byrne had once handed the surprised Harlem Hurricane, removed from the mind of the tramp the last vestige of any thought he might have harbored to do the newcomer bodily injury, and with it removed all else from the man's mind, temporarily.

As the fellow slumped, unconscious, to the ground, the camper rose to his feet.

"Some wallop you have concealed in your sleeve, my friend," he said; "place it there!" and he extended a slender, shapely hand.

Billy took it and shook it.

"It don't get under the ribs like those verses of yours, though, bo," he returned.

"It seems to have insinuated itself beneath this guy's thick skull," replied the poetical one, "and it's a cinch my verses, nor any other would ever get there."

The tramp who had plumbed the depths of the creek's foot of water and two feet of soft mud was crawling ashore.

"Whadda *you* want now?" inquired Billy Byrne. "A piece o' soap?"

"I'll get youse yet," spluttered the moist one through his watery whiskers.

"Ferget it," admonished Billy, "an' hit the trail." He pointed toward the railroad right of way. "An' you, too, John L," he added turning to the other victim of his artistic execution, who was now sitting up. "Hike!"

Mumbling and growling the two unwashed shuffled away, and were presently lost to view along the vanishing track.

The solitary camper had returned to his culinary effort, as unruffled and unconcerned, apparently, as though naught had occurred to disturb his peaceful solitude.

"Sit down," he said after a moment, looking up at Billy, "and have a bite to eat with me. Take that leather easy chair. The Louis Quatorze is too small and spindle-legged for comfort." He waved his hand invitingly toward the sward beside the fire.

For a moment he was entirely absorbed in the roasting fowl impaled upon a sharp stick which he held in his right hand. Then he presently broke again into verse.

Around the world and back again; we saw it all. The mist and rain

In England and the hot old plain from Needles
　　to Berdoo.
We kept a-rambling all the time. I rustled grub, he
　　rustled rhyme —
Blind-baggage, hoof it, ride or climb — we always
　　put it through.

"You're a good sort," he broke off, suddenly. "There
ain't many boes that would have done as much for a
fellow."

"It was two against one," replied Billy, "an' I don't
like them odds. Besides I like your poetry. Where d'ye
get it — make it up?"

"Lord, no," laughed the other. "If I could do that I
wouldn't be pan-handling. A guy by the name of Henry
Herbert Knibbs did them. Great, ain't they?"

"They sure is. They get me right where I live," and
then, after a pause; "sure you got enough fer two, bo?"

"I have enough for you, old top," replied the host,
"even if I only had half as much as I have. Here, take
first crack at the ambrosia. Sorry I have but a single
cup; but James has broken the others. James is very
careless. Sometimes I almost feel that I shall have to
let him go."

"Who's James?" asked Billy.

"James? Oh, James is my man," replied the other.

Billy looked up at his companion quizzically, then
he tasted the dark, thick concoction in the tin can.

"This is coffee," he announced. "I thought you said
it was ambrose."

"I only wished to see if you would recognize it, my
friend," replied the poetical one politely. "I am highly
complimented that you can guess what it is from its
taste."

For several minutes the two ate in silence, passing
the tin can back and forth, and slicing — hacking would

be more nearly correct — pieces of meat from the half-roasted fowl. It was Billy who broke the silence.

"I think," said he, "that you been stringin' me — 'bout James and ambrose."

The other laughed good-naturedly.

"You are not offended, I hope," said he. "This is a sad old world, you know, and we're all looking for amusement. If a guy has no money to buy it with, he has to manufacture it."

"Sure, I ain't sore," Billy assured him. "Say, spiel that part again 'bout Penelope with the kisses on her mouth, an' you can kid me till the cows come home."

The camper by the creek did as Billy asked him, while the latter sat with his eyes upon the fire seeing in the sputtering little flames the oval face of her who was Penelope to him.

When the verse was completed he reached forth his hand and took the tin can in his strong fingers, raising it before his face.

"Here's to — to his Knibbs!" he said, and drank, passing the battered thing over to his new friend.

"Yes," said the other; "here's to his Knibbs, and — Penelope!"

"Drink hearty," returned Billy Byrne.

The poetical one drew a sack of tobacco from his hip pocket and a rumpled package of papers from the pocket of his shirt, extending both toward Billy.

"Want the makings?" he asked.

"I ain't stuck on sponging," said Billy; "but maybe I can get even some day, and I sure do want a smoke. You see I was frisked. I ain't got nothin' — they didn't leave me a sou markee."

Billy reached across one end of the fire for the tobacco and cigarette papers. As he did so the movement bared his wrist, and as the firelight fell upon it the marks of the steel bracelet showed vividly. In the fall from the train the metal had bitten into the flesh.

His companion's eyes happened to fall upon the telltale mark. There was an almost imperceptible raising of the man's eyebrows; but he said nothing to indicate that he had noticed anything out of the ordinary.

The two smoked on for many minutes without indulging in conversation. The camper quoted snatches from Service and Kipling, then he came back to Knibbs, who was evidently his favorite. Billy listened and thought.

"Goin' anywheres in particular?" he asked during a momentary lull in the recitation.

"Oh, south or west," replied the other. "Nowhere in particular — any place suits me just so it isn't north or east."

"That's me," said Billy.

"Let's travel double, then," said the poetical one. "My name's Bridge."

"And mine's Billy. Here, shake," and Byrne extended his hand.

"Until one of us gets wearied of the other's company," said Bridge.

"You're on," replied Billy. "Let's turn in."

"Good," exclaimed Bridge. "I wonder what's keeping James. He should have been here long since to turn down my bed and fix my bath."

Billy grinned and rolled over on his side, his head uphill and his feet toward the fire. A couple of feet away Bridge paralleled him, and in five minutes both were breathing deeply in healthy slumber.

Chapter III

"FIVE HUNDRED DOLLARS REWARD"

"We kept a-rambling all the time. I rustled grub, he rustled rhyme,'" quoted Billy Byrne, sitting up and stretching himself.

His companion roused and came to one elbow. The sun was topping the scant wood behind them, glinting on the surface of the little creek. A robin hopped about the sward quite close to them, and from the branch of a tree a hundred yards away came the sweet piping of a song bird. Farther off were the distance-subdued noises of an awakening farm. The lowing of cows, the crowing of a rooster, the yelping of a happy dog just released from a night of captivity.

Bridge yawned and stretched. Billy rose to his feet and shook himself.

"This is the life," said Bridge. "Where you going?"

"To rustle grub," replied Billy. "That's my part o' the sketch."

The other laughed. "Go to it," he said. "I hate it. That's the part that has come nearest making me turn respectable than any other. I hate to ask for a hand-out."

Billy shrugged. He'd done worse things than that in his life, and off he trudged, whistling. He felt happier than he had for many a day. He never had guessed that the country in the morning could be so beautiful.

Behind him his companion collected the material for a fire, washed himself in the creek, and set the tin can, filled with water, at the edge of the kindling, and waited. There was nothing to cook, so it was useless to light the fire. As he sat there, thinking, his mind reverted to the red mark upon Billy's wrist, and he made a wry face.

Billy approached the farmhouse from which the sounds of awakening still emanated. The farmer saw him coming, and ceasing his activities about the barn-yard, leaned across a gate and eyed him, none too hospitably.

"I wanna get something to eat," explained Billy.

"Got any money to pay for it with?" asked the farmer quickly.

"No," said Billy; "but me partner an' me are hungry, an' we gotta eat."

The farmer extended a gnarled forefinger and pointed toward the rear of the house. Billy looked in the direction thus indicated and espied a woodpile. He grinned good naturedly.

Without a word he crossed to the corded wood, picked up an ax which was stuck in a chopping block, and, shedding his coat, went to work. The farmer resumed his chores. Half an hour later he stopped on his way in to breakfast and eyed the growing pile that lay beside Billy.

"You don't hev to chop all the wood in the county

to get a meal from Jed Watson," he said.

"I wanna get enough for me partner, too," explained Billy.

"Well, yew've chopped enough fer two meals, son," replied the farmer, and turning toward the kitchen door, he called: "Here, Maw, fix this boy up with suthin' t'eat — enough fer a couple of meals fer two on 'em."

As Billy walked away toward his camp, his arms laden with milk, butter, eggs, a loaf of bread and some cold meat, he grinned rather contentedly.

"A year or so ago," he mused, "I'd a stuck 'em up fer this, an' thought I was smart. Funny how a feller'll change — an' all fer a skirt. A skirt that belongs to somebody else now, too. Hell! what's the difference, anyhow? She'd be glad if she knew, an' it makes me feel better to act like she'd want. That old farmer guy, now. Who'd ever have taken him fer havin' a heart at all? Wen I seen him first I thought he'd like to sic the dog on me, an' there he comes along an' tells 'Maw' to pass me a hand-out like this! Gee! it's a funny world. She used to say that most everybody was decent if you went at 'em right, an' I guess she knew. She knew most everything, anyway. Lord, I wish she'd been born on Grand Ave., or I on Riverside Drive!"

As Billy walked up to his waiting companion, who had touched a match to the firewood as he sighted the numerous packages in the forager's arms, he was repeating, over and over, as though the words held him in the thrall of fascination: "There ain't no sweet Penelope somewhere that's longing much for me."

Bridge eyed the packages as Billy deposited them carefully and one at a time upon the grass beside the fire. The milk was in a clean little graniteware pail, the eggs had been placed in a paper bag, while the other articles were wrapped in pieces of newspaper.

As the opening of each revealed its contents, fresh, clean, and inviting, Bridge closed one eye and cocked the other up at Billy.

"Did he die hard?" he inquired.

"Did who die hard?" demanded the other.

"Why the dog, of course."

"He ain't dead as I know of," replied Billy.

"You don't mean to say, my friend, that they let you get away with all this without sicing the dog on you," said Bridge.

Billy laughed and explained, and the other was relieved — the red mark around Billy's wrist persisted in remaining uppermost in Bridge's mind.

When they had eaten they lay back upon the grass and smoked some more of Bridge's tobacco.

"Well," inquired Bridge, "what's doing now?"

"Let's be hikin'," said Billy.

Bridge rose and stretched. "'My feet are tired and need a change. Come on! It's up to you!'" he quoted.

Billy gathered together the food they had not yet eaten, and made two equal-sized packages of it. He handed one to Bridge.

"We'll divide the pack," he explained, "and here, drink the rest o' this milk, I want the pail."

"What are you going to do with the pail?" asked Bridge.

"Return it," said Billy. "'Maw' just loaned it to me."

Bridge elevated his eyebrows a trifle. He had been mistaken, after all. At the farmhouse the farmer's wife greeted them kindly, thanked Billy for returning her pail — which, if the truth were known, she had not expected to see again — and gave them each a handful of thick, light, golden-brown cookies, the tops of which were encrusted with sugar.

As they walked away Bridge sighed. "Nothing on earth like a good woman," he said.

"'Maw,' or 'Penelope'?" asked Billy.

"Either, or both," replied Bridge. "I have no Penelope, but I did have a mighty fine 'maw'."

Billy made no reply. He was thinking of the slovenly, blear-eyed woman who had brought him into the world. The memory was far from pleasant. He tried to shake it off.

"'Bridge,'" he said, quite suddenly, and apropos of nothing, in an effort to change the subject. "That's an odd name. I've heard of Bridges and Bridger; but I never heard Bridge before."

"Just a name a fellow gave me once up on the Yukon," explained Bridge. "I used to use a few words he'd never heard before, so he called me 'The Un-abridged,' which was too long. The fellows shortened it to 'Bridge' and it stuck. It has always stuck, and now I haven't any other. I even think of myself, now, as Bridge. Funny, ain't it?"

"Yes," agreed Billy, and that was the end of it. He never thought of asking his companion's true name, any more than Bridge would have questioned him as to his, or of his past. The ethics of the roadside fire and the empty tomato tin do not countenance such impertinences.

For several days the two continued their leisurely way toward Kansas City. Once they rode a few miles on a freight train, but for the most part they were content to plod joyously along the dusty highways. Billy continued to "rustle grub," while Bridge relieved the monotony by an occasional burst of poetry.

"You know so much of that stuff," said Billy as they were smoking by their camp fire one evening, "that I'd think you'd be able to make some up yourself."

"I've tried," admitted Bridge; "but there always seems to be something lacking in my stuff — it don't get under your belt — the divine afflatus is not there. I may start out all right, but I always end up where I didn't expect to go, and where nobody wants to be."

"'Member any of it?" asked Billy.

"There was one I wrote about a lake where I camped once," said Bridge, reminiscently; "but I can only recall one stanza."

"Let's have it," urged Billy. "I bet it has Knibbs hangin' to the ropes."

Bridge cleared his throat, and recited:

Silver are the ripples,
Solemn are the dunes,
Happy are the fishes,
For they are full of prunes.

He looked up at Billy, a smile twitching at the corners of his mouth. "How's that?" he asked.

Billy scratched his head.

"It's all right but the last line," said Billy, candidly. "There is something wrong with that last line."

"Yes," agreed Bridge, "there is."

"I guess Knibbs is safe for another round at least," said Billy.

Bridge was eying his companion, noting the broad shoulders, the deep chest, the mighty forearm and biceps which the other's light cotton shirt could not conceal.

"It is none of my business," he said presently; "but from your general appearance, from bits of idiom you occasionally drop, and from the way you handled those two boes the night we met I should rather surmise that at some time or other you had been less than a thousand miles from the w.k. roped arena."

"I seen a prize fight once," admitted Billy.

It was the day before they were due to arrive in Kansas City that Billy earned a hand-out from a restaurant keeper in a small town by doing some odd jobs for the man. The food he gave Billy was wrapped in an old copy of the Kansas City Star. When Billy reached camp he tossed the package to Bridge, who, in addition to his honorable post as poet laureate, was also cook. Then Billy walked down to the stream, near-by, that he might wash away the grime and sweat of honest toil from his hands and face.

As Bridge unwrapped the package and the paper unfolded beneath his eyes an article caught his attention — just casually at first; but presently to the exclusion of all else. As he read his eyebrows alternated between a position of considerable elevation to that of a deep frown. Occasionally he nodded knowingly. Finally he glanced up at Billy who was just rising from his ablutions. Hastily Bridge tore from the paper the article that had attracted his interest, folded it, and stuffed it into one of his pockets — he had not had time to finish the reading and he wanted to save the article for a later opportunity for careful perusal.

That evening Bridge sat for a long time scrutinizing Billy through half-closed lids, and often he found his eyes wandering to the red ring about the other's wrist; but whatever may have been within his thoughts he kept to himself.

It was noon when the two sauntered into Kansas City. Billy had a dollar in his pocket — a whole dollar. He had earned it assisting an automobilist out of a ditch.

"We'll have a swell feed," he had confided to Bridge, "an' sleep in a bed just to learn how much nicer it is sleepin' out under the black sky and the shiny little stars."

"You're a profligate, Billy," said Bridge.

"I dunno what that means," said Billy; "but if it's something I shouldn't be I probably am."

The two went to a rooming-house of which Bridge knew, where they could get a clean room with a double bed for fifty cents. It was rather a high price to pay, of course, but Bridge was more or less fastidious, and he admitted to Billy that he'd rather sleep in the clean dirt of the roadside than in the breed of dirt one finds in an unclean bed.

At the end of the hall was a washroom, and toward this Bridge made his way, after removing his coat and throwing it across the foot of the bed. After he had left the room Billy chanced to notice a folded bit of newspaper on the floor beneath Bridge's coat. He picked it up to lay it on the little table which answered the purpose of a dresser when a single word caught his attention. It was a name: Schneider.

Billy unfolded the clipping and as his eyes took in the heading a strange expression entered them — a hard, cold gleam such as had not touched them since the day that he abandoned the deputy sheriff in the woods midway between Chicago and Joliet.

This is what Billy read:

Billy Byrne, sentenced to life imprisonment in Joliet penitentiary for the murder of Schneider, the old West Side saloon keeper, hurled himself from the train that was bearing him to Joliet yesterday, dragging with him the deputy sheriff to whom he was handcuffed.

The deputy was found a few hours later bound and gagged, lying in the woods along the Santa Fe, not far from Lemont. He was uninjured. He says that Byrne got a good start, and doubtless took advantage of it to return to Chicago, where a man of his stamp could find more numerous and safer retreats than elsewhere.

There was much more — a detailed account of the crime for the commission of which Billy had been sentenced, a full and complete description of Billy, a record of his long years of transgression, and, at last, the mention of a five-hundred-dollar reward that the authorities had offered for information that would lead to his arrest.

When Billy had concluded the reading he refolded the paper and placed it in a pocket of the coat hanging upon the foot of the bed. A moment later Bridge entered the room. Billy caught himself looking often at his companion, and always there came to his mind the termination of the article he had found in Bridge's pocket — the mention of the five-hundred-dollar reward.

"Five hundred dollars," thought Billy, "is a lot o' coin. I just wonder now," and he let his eyes wander to his companion as though he might read upon his face the purpose which lay in the man's heart. "He don't look it; but five hundred dollars is a lot o' coin — fer a bo, and wotinell did he have that article hid in his clothes fer? That's wot I'd like to know. I guess it's up to me to blow."

All the recently acquired content which had been Billy's since he had come upon the poetic Bridge and the two had made their carefree, leisurely way along shaded country roadsides, or paused beside cool brooklets that meandered lazily through sweet-smelling meadows, was dissipated in the instant that he had realized the nature of the article his companion had been carrying and hiding from him.

For days no thought of pursuit or capture had arisen to perplex him. He had seemed such a tiny thing out there amidst the vastness of rolling hills, of woods, and plain that there had been induced within him an unconscious assurance that no one could find him even though they might seek for him.

The idea of meeting a plain clothes man from detective headquarters around the next bend of a peaceful Missouri road was so preposterous and incongruous that Billy had found it impossible to give the matter serious thought.

He never before had been in the country districts of his native land. To him the United States was all like Chicago or New York or Milwaukee, the three cities with which he was most familiar. His experience of unurban localities had been gained amidst the primeval jungles of far-away Yoka. There had been no detective sergeants there — unquestionably there could be none here. Detective sergeants were indigenous to the soil that grew corner saloons and poolrooms, and to none other — as well expect to discover one of Oda Yorimoto's samurai hiding behind a fire plug on Michigan Boulevard, as to look for one of those others along a farm-bordered road.

But here in Kansas City, amidst the noises and odors that meant a large city, it was different. Here the next man he met might be looking for him, or if not then the very first policeman they encountered could arrest him upon a word from Bridge — and Bridge would get five hundred dollars. Just then Bridge burst forth into poetry:

In a flannel shirt from earth's clean dirt,
    Here, pal, is my calloused hand!
Oh, I love each day as a rover may,
    Nor seek to understand.
To enjoy is good enough for me;
    The gypsy of God am I.
Then here's a hail to —

"Say," he interrupted himself; "what's the matter

with going out now and wrapping ourselves around that swell feed you were speaking of?"

Billy rose. It didn't seem possible that Bridge could be going to double-cross him.

In a flannel shirt from earth's clean dirt,
Here, pal, is my calloused hand!

Billy repeated the lines half aloud. They renewed his confidence in Bridge, somehow.

"Like them?" asked the latter.

"Yes," said Billy; "s'more of Knibbs?"

"No, Service. Come on, let's go and dine. How about the Midland?" and he grinned at his little joke as he led the way toward the street.

It was late afternoon. The sun already had set; but it still was too light for lamps. Bridge led the way toward a certain eating-place of which he knew where a man might dine well and from a clean platter for two bits. Billy had been keeping his eyes open for detectives. They had passed no uniformed police — that would be the crucial test, thought he — unless Bridge intended tipping off headquarters on the quiet and having the pinch made at night after Billy had gone to bed.

As they reached the little restaurant, which was in a basement, Bridge motioned Billy down ahead of him. Just for an instant he, himself, paused at the head of the stairs and looked about. As he did so a man stepped from the shadow of a doorway upon the opposite side of the street.

If Bridge saw him he apparently gave no sign, for he turned slowly and with deliberate steps followed Billy down into the eating-place.

Chapter IV

ON THE TRAIL

As they entered the place Billy, who was ahead, sought a table; but as he was about to hang up his cap and seat himself Bridge touched his elbow.

"Let's go to the washroom and clean up a bit," he said, in a voice that might be heard by those nearest.

"Why, we just washed before we left our room," expostulated Billy.

"Shut up and follow me," Bridge whispered into his ear.

Immediately Billy was all suspicion. His hand flew to the pocket in which the gun of the deputy sheriff still rested. They would never take him alive, of that Billy was positive. He wouldn't go back to life imprisonment, not after he had tasted the sweet freedom of the wide spaces — such a freedom as the trammeled city cannot offer.

Bridge saw the movement.

"Cut it," he whispered, "and follow me, as I tell you. I just saw a Chicago dick across the street. He may not have seen you, but it looked almighty like it. He'll be down here in about two seconds now. Come on — we'll beat it through the rear — I know the way."

Billy Byrne heaved a great sigh of relief. Suddenly he was almost reconciled to the thought of capture, for in the instant he had realized that it had not been so much his freedom that he had dreaded to lose as his faith in the companion in whom he had believed.

Without sign of haste the two walked the length of the room and disappeared through the doorway leading into the washroom. Before them was a window opening upon a squalid back yard. The building stood upon a hillside, so that while the entrance to the eating-place was below the level of the street in front, its rear was flush with the ground.

Bridge motioned Billy to climb through the window while he shot the bolt upon the inside of the door leading back into the restaurant. A moment later he followed the fugitive, and then took the lead.

Down narrow, dirty alleys, and through litter-piled back yards he made his way, while Billy followed at his heels. Dusk was gathering, and before they had gone far darkness came.

They neither paused nor spoke until they had left the business portion of the city behind and were well out of the zone of bright lights. Bridge was the first to break the silence.

"I suppose you wonder how I knew," he said.

"No," replied Billy. "I seen that clipping you got in your pocket — it fell out on the floor when you took your coat off in the room this afternoon to go and wash."

"Oh," said Bridge, "I see. Well, as far as I'm concerned that's the end of it — we won't mention it again, old man. I don't need to tell you that I'm for you."

"No, not after tonight," Billy assured him.

They went on again for some little time without speaking, then Billy said:

"I got two things to tell you. The first is that after I seen that newspaper article in your clothes I thought you was figurin' on double-crossin' me an' claimin' the five hun. I ought to of known better. The other is that I didn't kill Schneider. I wasn't near his place that night — an' that's straight."

"I'm glad you told me both," said Bridge. "I think we'll understand each other better after this — we're each runnin' away from something. We'll run together, eh?" and he extended his hand. "In flannel shirt from earth's clean dirt, here, pal, is my calloused hand!" he quoted, laughing.

Billy took the other's hand. He noticed that Bridge hadn't said what *he* was running away from. Billy wondered; but asked no questions.

South they went after they had left the city behind, out into the sweet and silent darkness of the country. During the night they crossed the line into Kansas, and morning found them in a beautiful, hilly country to which all thoughts of cities, crime, and police seemed so utterly foreign that Billy could scarce believe that only a few hours before a Chicago detective had been less than a hundred feet from him.

The new sun burst upon them as they topped a grassy hill. The dew-bespangled blades scintillated beneath the gorgeous rays which would presently sweep them away again into the nothingness from which they had sprung.

Bridge halted and stretched himself. He threw his head back and let the warm sun beat down upon his bronzed face.

There's sunshine in the heart of me,
My blood sings in the breeze;

The mountains are a part of me,
I'm fellow to the trees.
My golden youth I'm squandering,
Sun-libertine am I,
A-wandering, a-wandering,
Until the day I die.

And then he stood for minutes drinking in deep breaths of the pure, sweet air of the new day. Beside him, a head taller, savagely strong, stood Billy Byrne, his broad shoulders squared, his great chest expanding as he inhaled.

"It's great, ain't it?" he said, at last. "I never knew the country was like this, an' I don't know that I ever would have known it if it hadn't been for those poet guys you're always spouting.

"I always had an idea they was sissy fellows," he went on; "but a guy can't be a sissy an' think the thoughts they musta thought to write stuff that sends the blood chasin' through a feller like he'd had a drink on an empty stomach.

"I used to think everybody was a sissy who wasn't a tough guy. I was a tough guy all right, an' I was mighty proud of it. I ain't any more an' haven't been for a long time; but before I took a tumble to myself I'd have hated you, Bridge. I'd a-hated your fine talk, an' your poetry, an' the thing about you that makes you hate to touch a guy for a hand-out.

"I'd a-hated myself if I'd thought that I could ever talk mushy like I am now. Gee, Bridge, but I was the limit! A girl — a nice girl — called me a mucker once, an' a coward. I was both; but I had the reputation of bein' the toughest guy on the West Side, an' I thought I was a man. I nearly poked her face for her — think of it, Bridge! I nearly did; but something stopped me — something held my hand from it, an' lately I've liked to think that maybe what stopped me was something in me that had always been there — something decent that was really a part of me. I hate to think that I was such a beast at heart as I acted like all my life up to that minute. I began to change then. It was mighty slow, an' I'm still a roughneck; but I'm gettin' on. She helped me most, of course, an' now you're helpin' me a lot, too — you an' your poetry stuff. If some dick don't get me I may get to be a human bein' before I die."

Bridge laughed.

"It *is* odd," he said, "how our viewpoints change with changed environment and the passing of the years. Time was, Billy, when I'd have hated you as much as you would have hated me. I don't know that I should have said hate, for that is not exactly the word. It was more contempt that I felt for men whom I considered as not belonging upon that intellectual or social plane to which I considered I had been born.

"I thought of people who moved outside my limited sphere as 'the great unwashed.' I pitied them, and I honestly believe now that in the bottom of my heart I considered them of different clay than I, and with souls, if they possessed such things, about on a par with the souls of sheep and cows.

"I couldn't have seen the man in you, Billy, then, any more than you could have seen the man in me. I have learned much since then, though I still stick to a part of my original articles of faith — I do believe that all men are not equal; and I know that there are a great many more with whom I would not pal than there are those with whom I would.

"Because one man speaks better English than another, or has read more and remembers it, only makes him a better man in that particular respect. I think none the less of you because you can't quote Browning or Shakespeare — the thing that counts is that you can appreciate, as I do, Service and Kipling and Knibbs.

"Now maybe we are both wrong — maybe Knibbs and Kipling and Service didn't write poetry, and some people will say as much; but whatever it is it gets you and me in the same way, and so in this respect we are equals. Which being the case let's see if we can't rustle some grub, and then find a nice soft spot whereon to pound our respective ears."

Billy, deciding that he was too sleepy to work for food, invested half of the capital that was to have furnished the swell feed the night before in what two bits would purchase from a generous housewife on a near-by farm, and then, stretching themselves beneath the shade of a tree sufficiently far from the road that they might not attract unnecessary observation, they slept until after noon.

But their precaution failed to serve their purpose entirely. A little before noon two filthy, bearded knights of the road clambered laboriously over the fence and headed directly for the very tree under which Billy and Bridge lay sleeping. In the minds of the two was the same thought that had induced Billy Byrne and the poetic Bridge to seek this same secluded spot.

There was in the stiff shuffle of the men something rather familiar. We have seen them before — just for a few minutes it is true; but under circumstances that impressed some of their characteristics upon us. The very last we saw of them they were shuffling away in the darkness along a railroad track, after promising that eventually they would wreak dire vengeance upon Billy, who had just trounced them.

Now as they came unexpectedly upon the two sleepers they did not immediately recognize in them the objects of their recent hate. They just stood looking stupidly down on them, wondering in what way they might turn their discovery to their own advantage.

Nothing in the raiment either of Billy or Bridge indicated that here was any particularly rich field for loot, and, too, the athletic figure of Byrne would rather have discouraged any attempt to roll him without first handing him the "k.o.," as the two would have naively put it.

But as they gazed down upon the features of the sleepers the eyes of one of the tramps narrowed to two ugly slits while those of his companion went wide in incredulity and surprise.

"Do youse know dem guys?" asked the first, and without waiting for a reply he went on: "Dem's de guys dat beat us up back dere de udder side o' K. C. Do youse get 'em?"

"Sure?" asked the other.

"Sure, I'd know dem in a t'ous'n'. Le's hand 'em a couple an' beat it," and he stooped to pick up a large stone that lay near at hand.

"Cut it!" whispered the second tramp. "Youse don't know dem guys at all. Dey may be de guys dat beats us up; but dat big stiff dere is more dan dat. He's wanted in Chi, an' dere's half a t'ou on 'im."

"Who put youse jerry to all dat?" inquired the first tramp, skeptically.

"I was in de still wit 'im — he croaked some guy. He's a lifer. On de way to de pen he pushes dis dick off'n de rattler an' makes his get-away. Dat peter-boy we meets at Quincy slips me an earful about him. Here's w'ere we draws down de five hundred if we're cagey."

"Whaddaya mean, cagey?"

"Why we leaves 'em alone an' goes to de nex' farm an' calls up K. C. an' tips off de dicks, see?"

"Youse don't tink we'll get any o' dat five hun, do youse, wit de dicks in on it?"

The other scratched his head.

"No," he said, rather dubiously, after a moment's deep thought; "dey don't nobody get nothin' dat de dicks see first; but we'll get even with dese blokes, anyway."

"Maybe dey'll pass us a couple bucks," said the other hopefully. "Dey'd orter do dat much."

Detective Sergeant Flannagan of Headquarters, Chicago, slouched in a chair in the private office of the chief of detectives of Kansas City, Missouri. Sergeant Flannagan was sore. He would have said as much himself. He had been sent west to identify a suspect whom the Kansas City authorities had arrested; but had been unable to do so, and had been preparing to return to his home city when the brilliant aureola of an unusual piece of excellent fortune had shone upon him for a moment, and then faded away through the grimy entrance of a basement eating-place.

He had been walking along the street the previous evening thinking of nothing in particular; but with eyes and ears alert as becomes a successful police officer, when he had espied two men approaching upon the opposite sidewalk.

There was something familiar in the swing of the giant frame of one of the men. So, true to years of training, Sergeant Flannagan melted into the shadows of a store entrance and waited until the two should have come closer.

They were directly opposite him when the truth flashed upon him — the big fellow was Billy Byrne, and there was a five-hundred-dollar reward out for him.

And then the two turned and disappeared down the stairway that led to the underground restaurant. Sergeant Flannagan saw Byrne's companion turn and look back just as Flannagan stepped from the doorway to cross the street after them.

That was the last Sergeant Flannagan had seen either

of Billy Byrne or his companion. The trail had ceased
at the open window of the washroom at the rear of the
restaurant, and search as he would he had been unable
to pick it up again.

No one in Kansas City had seen two men that night
answering the descriptions Flannagan had been able
to give — at least no one whom Flannagan could
unearth.

Finally he had been forced to take the Kansas City
chief into his confidence, and already a dozen men
were scouring such sections of Kansas City in which
it seemed most likely an escaped murderer would
choose to hide.

Flannagan had been out himself for a while; but now
he was in to learn what progress, if any, had been made.
He had just learned that three suspects had been arrested and was waiting to have them paraded before
him.

When the door swung in and the three were escorted
into his presence Sergeant Flannagan gave a snort of
disgust, indicative probably not only of despair; but in
a manner registering his private opinion of the mental
horse power and efficiency of the Kansas City sleuths,
for of the three one was a pasty-faced, chestless youth,
even then under the influence of cocaine, another was
an old, bewhiskered hobo, while the third was unquestionably a Chinaman.

Even professional courtesy could scarce restrain Sergeant Flannagan's desire toward bitter sarcasm, and he
was upon the point of launching forth into a vitriolic
arraignment of everything west of Chicago up to and
including, specifically, the Kansas City detective bu-
reau, when the telephone bell at the chief's desk interrupted him. He had wanted the chief to hear just what
he thought, so he waited.

The chief listened for a few minutes, asked several

questions and then, placing a fat hand over the transmitter, he wheeled about toward Flannagan.

"Well," he said, "I guess I got something for you at last. There's a bo on the wire that says he's just seen your man down near Shawnee. He wants to know if you'll split the reward with him."

Flannagan yawned and stretched.

"I suppose," he said, ironically, "that if I go down there I'll find he's corralled a nigger," and he looked sorrowfully at the three specimens before him.

"I dunno," said the chief. "This guy says he knows Byrne well, an' that he's got it in for him. Shall I tell him you'll be down — and split the reward?"

"Tell him I'll be down and that I'll treat him right," replied Flannagan, and after the chief had transmitted the message, and hung up the receiver: "Where is this here Shawnee, anyhow?"

"I'll send a couple of men along with you. It isn't far across the line, an' there won't be no trouble in getting back without nobody knowin' anything about it — if you get him."

"All right," said Flannagan, his visions of five hundred already dwindled to a possible one.

It was but a little past one o'clock that a touring car rolled south out of Kansas City with Detective Sergeant Flannagan in the front seat with the driver and two burly representatives of Missouri law in the back.

Chapter V

ONE TURN DESERVES ANOTHER

*W*hen the two tramps approached the farmhouse at which Billy had purchased food a few hours before the farmer's wife called the dog that was asleep in the summer kitchen and took a shotgun down from its hook beside the door.

From long experience the lady was a reader of character — of hobo character at least — and she saw nothing in the appearance of either of these two that inspired even a modicum of confidence. Now the young fellow who had been there earlier in the day and who, wonder of wonders, had actually paid for the food she gave him, had been of a different stamp. His clothing had proclaimed him a tramp, but, thanks to the razor Bridge always carried, he was clean shaven. His year of total abstinence bad given him clear eyes and a healthy skin. There was a freshness and vigor in his appearance and carriage that inspired confidence rather than suspicion.

She had not mistrusted him; but these others she did mistrust. When they asked to use the telephone she refused and ordered them away, thinking it but an excuse to enter the house; but they argued the matter, explaining that they had discovered an escaped murderer hiding near — by — in fact in her own meadow — and that they wished only to call up the Kansas City police.

Finally she yielded, but kept the dog by her side and the shotgun in her hand while the two entered the room and crossed to the telephone upon the opposite side.

From the conversation which she overheard the woman concluded that, after all, she had been mistaken, not only about these two, but about the young man who had come earlier in the day and purchased food from her, for the description the tramp gave of the fugitive tallied exactly with that of the young man.

It seemed incredible that so honest looking a man could be a murderer. The good woman was shocked, and not a little unstrung by the thought that she had been in the house alone when he had come and that if he had wished to he could easily have murdered her.

"I hope they get him," she said, when the tramp had concluded his talk with Kansas City. "It's awful the carryings on they is nowadays. Why a body can't never tell who to trust, and I thought him such a nice young man. And he paid me for what he got, too."

The dog, bored by the inaction, had wandered back into the summer kitchen and resumed his broken slumber. One of the tramps was leaning against the wall talking with the farmer woman. The other was busily engaged in scratching his right shin with what remained of the heel of his left shoe. He supported himself with one hand on a small table upon the top of which was a family Bible.

Quite unexpectedly he lost his balance, the table tipped, he was thrown still farther over toward it, and all in the flash of an eye tramp, table, and family Bible crashed to the floor.

With a little cry of alarm the woman rushed forward to gather up the Holy Book, in her haste forgetting the shotgun and leaving it behind her leaning against the arm of a chair.

Almost simultaneously the two tramps saw the real cause of her perturbation. The large book had fallen upon its back, open; and as several of the leaves turned over before coming to rest their eyes went wide at what was revealed between.

United States currency in denominations of five, ten, and twenty-dollar bills lay snugly inserted between the leaves of the Bible. The tramp who lay on the floor, as yet too surprised to attempt to rise, rolled over and seized the book as a football player seizes the pigskin after a fumble, covering it with his body, his arms, and sticking out his elbows as a further protection to the invaluable thing.

At the first cry of the woman the dog rose, growling, and bounded into the room. The tramp leaning against the wall saw the brute coming — a mongrel hound-dog, bristling and savage.

The shotgun stood almost within the man's reach — a step and it was in his hands. As though sensing the fellow's intentions the dog wheeled from the tramp upon the floor, toward whom he had leaped, and sprang for the other ragged scoundrel.

The muzzle of the gun met him halfway. There was a deafening roar. The dog collapsed to the floor, his chest torn out. Now the woman began to scream for help; but in an instant both the tramps were upon her choking her to silence.

One of them ran to the summer kitchen, returning a moment later with a piece of clothesline, while the other sat astride the victim, his fingers closed about her throat. Once he released his hold and she screamed again. Presently she was secured and gagged. Then the two commenced to rifle the Bible.

Eleven hundred dollars in bills were hidden there, because the woman and her husband didn't believe in banks — the savings of a lifetime. In agony, as she regained consciousness, she saw the last of their little hoard transferred to the pockets of the tramps, and when they had finished they demanded to know where she kept the rest, loosening her gag that she might reply.

She told them that that was all the money she had in the world, and begged them not to take it.

"Youse've got more coin dan dis," growled one of the men, "an' youse had better pass it over, or we'll find a way to make youse."

But still she insisted that that was all. The tramp stepped into the kitchen. A wood fire was burning in the stove. A pair of pliers lay upon the window sill. With these he lifted one of the hot stove-hole covers and returned to the parlor, grinning.

"I guess she'll remember she's got more wen dis begins to woik," he said. "Take off her shoes, Dink."

The other growled an objection.

"Yeh poor boob," he said. "De dicks'll be here in a little while. We'd better be makin' our get-away wid w'at we got."

"Gee!" exclaimed his companion. "I clean forgot all about de dicks," and then after a moment's silence during which his evil face underwent various changes of expression from fear to final relief, he turned an ugly, crooked grimace upon his companion.

"We got to croak her," he said. "Dey ain't no udder

way. If dey finds her alive she'll blab sure, an' dey won't be no trouble 'bout gettin' us or identifyin' us neither."

The other shrugged.

"Le's beat it," he whined. "We can't more'n do time fer dis job if we stop now; but de udder'll mean —" and he made a suggestive circle with a grimy finger close to his neck.

"No it won't nothin' of de kind," urged his companion. "I got it all doped out. We got lots o' time before de dicks are due. We'll croak de skirt, an' den we'll beat it up de road *an' meet de dicks* — see?"

The other was aghast.

"Wen did youse go nuts?" he asked.

"I ain't gone nuts. Wait 'til I gets t'rough. We meets de dicks, innocent-like; but first we caches de dough in de woods. We tells 'em we hurried right on to lead 'em to dis Byrne guy, an' wen we gets back here to de farmhouse an' finds wot's happened here we'll be as flabbergasted as dey be."

"Oh, nuts!" exclaimed the other disgustedly. "Youse don't tink youse can put dat over on any wise guy from Chi, do youse? Who will dey tink croaked de old woman an' de ki-yi? Will dey tink dey kilt deyreselves?"

"Dey'll tink Byrne an' his pardner croaked 'em, you simp," replied Crumb.

Dink scratched his head, and as the possibilities of the scheme filtered into his dull brain a broad grin bared his yellow teeth.

"You're dere, pal," he exclaimed, real admiration in his tone. "But who's goin' to do it?"

"I'll do it," said Crumb. "Dere ain't no chanct of gettin' in bad for it, so I jest as soon do the job. Get me a knife, or an ax from de kitchen — de gat makes too much noise."

Something awoke Billy Byrne with a start. Faintly, in the back of his consciousness, the dim suggestion of a loud noise still reverberated. He sat up and looked about him.

"I wonder what that was?" he mused. "It sounded like the report of a gun."

Bridge awoke about the same time, and turned lazily over, raising himself upon an elbow. He grinned at Billy.

"Good morning," he said, and then:

Says I, "Then let's be on the float. You certainly
      have got my goat;
You make me hungry in my throat for seeing things
      that's new.
Out there somewhere we'll ride the range a-looking
      for the new and strange;
My feet are tired and need a change. Come on! It's
      up to you!"

"Come on, then," agreed Billy, coming to his feet.

As he rose there came, faintly, but distinct, the un-mistakable scream of a frightened woman. From the direction of the farmhouse it came — from the farm-house at which Billy had purchased their breakfast.

Without waiting for a repetition of the cry Billy wheeled and broke into a rapid run in the direction of the little cluster of buildings. Bridge leaped to his feet and followed him, dropping behind though, for he had not had the road work that Billy recently had been through in his training for the battle in which he had defeated the "white hope" that time in New York when Professor Cassidy had wagered his entire pile upon him, nor in vain.

Dink searched about the summer kitchen for an ax

or hatchet; but failing to find either rummaged through a table drawer until he came upon a large carving knife. This would do the job nicely. He thumbed the edge as he carried it back into the parlor to Crumb.

The poor woman, lying upon the floor, was quite conscious. Her eyes were wide and rolling in horror. She struggled with her bonds, and tried to force the gag from her mouth with her tongue; but her every effort was useless. She had heard every word that had passed between the two men. She knew that they would carry out the plan they had formulated and that there was no chance that they would be interrupted in their gruesome work, for her husband had driven over to a farm beyond Holliday, leaving before sunrise, and there was little prospect that he would return before milking time in the evening. The detectives from Kansas City could not possibly reach the farm until far too late to save her.

She saw Dink return from the summer kitchen with the long knife. She recalled the day she had bought that knife in town, and the various uses to which she had put it. That very morning she had sliced some bacon with it. How distinctly such little things recurred to her at this frightful moment. And now the hideous creature standing beside her was going to use it to cut her throat.

She saw Crumb take the knife and feel of the blade, running his thumb along it. She saw him stoop, his eyes turned down upon hers. He grasped her chin and forced it upward and back, the better to expose her throat.

Oh, why could she not faint? Why must she suffer all these hideous preliminaries? Why could she not even close her eyes?

Crumb raised the knife and held the blade close

above her bared neck. A shudder ran through her, and then the door crashed open and a man sprang into the room. It was Billy Byrne. Through the window he had seen what was passing in the interior.

His hand fell upon Crumb's collar and jerked him backward from his prey. Dink seized the shotgun and turned it upon the intruder; but he was too close. Billy grasped the barrel of the weapon and threw the muzzle up toward the ceiling as the tramp pulled the trigger. Then he wrenched it from the man's hands, swung it once above his head and crashed the stock down upon Dink's skull.

Dink went down and out for the count — for several counts, in fact. Crumb stumbled to his feet and made a break for the door. In the doorway he ran full into Bridge, winded, but ready. The latter realizing that the matted one was attempting to escape, seized a handful of his tangled beard, and, as he had done upon another occasion, held the tramp's head in rigid position while he planted a series of blows in the fellow's face — blows that left Crumb as completely out of battle as was his mildewed comrade.

"Watch 'em," said Billy, handing Bridge the shotgun. Then he turned his attention to the woman. With the carving knife that was to have ended her life he cut her bonds. Removing the gag from her mouth he lifted her in his strong arms and carried her to the little horsehair sofa that stood in one corner of the parlor, laying her upon it very gently.

He was thinking of "Maw" Watson. This woman resembled her just a little — particularly in her comfortable, motherly expansiveness, and she had had a kind word and a cheery good-bye for him that morning as he had departed.

The woman lay upon the sofa, breathing hard, and moaning just a little. The shock had been almost too much even for her stolid nerves. Presently she turned her eyes toward Billy.

"You are a good boy," she said, "and you come just in the nick o' time. They got all my money. It's in their clothes," and then a look of terror overspread her face. For the moment she had forgotten what she had heard about this man — that he was an escaped convict — a convicted murderer. Was she any better off now that she had let him know about the money than she was with the others after they discovered it?

At her words Bridge kneeled and searched the two tramps. He counted the bills as he removed them from their pockets.

"Eleven hundred?" he asked, and handed the money to Billy.

"Eleven hundred, yes," breathed the woman, faintly, her eyes horror-filled and fearful as she gazed upon Billy's face. She didn't care for the money any more — they could have it all if they would only let her live.

Billy turned toward her and held the rumpled green mass out.

"Here," he said; "but that's an awful lot o' coin for a woman to have about de house — an' her all alone. You ought not to a-done it."

She took the money in trembling fingers. It seemed incredible that the man was returning it to her.

"But I knew it," she said finally.

"Knew what?" asked Billy.

"I knew you was a good boy. They said you was a murderer."

Billy's brows contracted, and an expression of pain crossed his face.

"How did they come to say that?" he asked.

"I heard them telephonin' to Kansas City to the police," she replied, and then she sat bolt upright. "The detectives are on their way here now," she almost screamed, "and even if you *are* a murderer I don't care. I won't stand by and see 'em get you after what you have done for me. I don't believe you're a murderer anyhow. You're a good boy. My boy would be about as old and as big as you by now — if he lives. He ran away a long time ago — maybe you've met him. His name's Eddie — Eddie Shorter. I ain't heard from him fer years.

"No," she went on, "I don't believe what they said — you got too good a face; but if you are a murderer you get out now before they come an' I'll send 'em on a wild-goose chase in the wrong direction."

"But these," said Billy. "We can't leave these here."

"Tie 'em up and give me the shotgun," she said. "I'll bet they don't come any more funny business on me." She had regained both her composure and her nerve by this time.

Together Billy and Bridge trussed up the two tramps. An elephant couldn't have forced the bonds they placed upon them. Then they carried them down cellar and when they had come up again Mrs. Shorter barred the cellar door.

"I reckon they won't get out of there very fast," she said. "And now you two boys run along. Got any money?" and without waiting for a reply she counted twenty-five dollars from the roll she had tucked in the front of her waist and handed them to Billy.

"Nothin' doin'," said he; "but t'anks just the same."

"You got to take it," she insisted. "Let me make believe I'm givin' it to my boy, Eddie — please," and the tears that came to her eyes proved far more effective than her generous words.

"Aw, all right," said Billy. "I'll take it an' pass it along to Eddie if I ever meet him, eh?"

"Now please hurry," she urged. "I don't want you to be caught — even if you are a murderer. I wish you weren't though."

"I'm not," said Billy; "but de law says I am an' what de law says, goes."

He turned toward the doorway with Bridge, calling a goodbye to the woman, but as he stepped out upon the veranda the dust of a fast-moving automobile appeared about a bend in the road a half-mile from the house.

"Too late," he said, turning to Bridge. "Here they come!"

The woman brushed by them and peered up the road.

"Yes," she said, "it must be them. Lordy! What'll we do?"

"I'll duck out the back way, that's what I'll do," said Billy.

"It wouldn't do a mite of good," said Mrs. Shorter, with a shake of her head. "They'll telephone every farmer within twenty mile of here in every direction, an' they'll get you sure. Wait! I got a scheme. Come with me," and she turned and bustled through the little parlor, out of a doorway into something that was half hall and half storeroom. There was a flight of stairs leading to the upper story, and she waddled up them as fast as her legs would carry her, motioning the two men to follow her.

In a rear room was a trapdoor in the ceiling.

"Drag that commode under this," she told them. "Then climb into the attic, and close the trapdoor. They won't never find you there."

Billy pulled the ancient article of furniture beneath the opening, and in another moment the two men were in the stuffy atmosphere of the unventilated loft. Beneath them they heard Mrs. Shorter dragging the commode back to its accustomed place, and then the sound of her footsteps descending the stair.

Presently there came to them the rattling of a motor without, followed by the voices of men in the house. For an hour, half asphyxiated by the closeness of the attic, they waited, and then again they heard the sound of the running engine, diminishing as the machine drew away.

Shortly after, Mrs. Shorter's voice rose to them from below:

"You ken come down now," she said, "they've gone."

When they had descended she led them to the kitchen.

"I got a bite to eat ready for you while they was here," she explained. "When you've done you ken hide in the barn 'til dark, an' after that I'll have my ol' man take you 'cross to Dodson, that's a junction, an' you'd aughter be able to git away easy enough from there. I told 'em you started for Olathe — there's where they've gone with the two tramps.

"My, but I did have a time of it! I ain't much good at story-tellin' but I reckon I told more stories this arternoon than I ever tole before in all my life. I told 'em that they was two of you, an' that the biggest one hed red hair, an' the little one was all pock-marked. Then they said you prob'ly wasn't the man at all, an' my! how they did swear at them two tramps fer gettin' 'em way out here on a wild-goose chase; but they're goin' to look fer you jes' the same in Olathe, only they won't find you there," and she laughed, a bit nervously though.

It was dusk when Mr. Shorter returned from Holliday, but after he had heard his wife's story he said that he'd drive "them two byes" all the way to Mexico, if there wasn't any better plan.

"Dodson's far enough," Bridge assured him, and late that night the grateful farmer set them down at their destination.

An hour later they were speeding south on the Missouri Pacific.

Bridge lay back, luxuriously, on the red plush of the smoker seat.

"Some class to us, eh, bo?" asked Billy.

Bridge stretched.

> The tide-hounds race far up the shore — the
> hunt is on! The breakers roar!
> Her spars are tipped with gold, and o'er her deck
> the spray is flung,
> The buoys that frolic in the bay, they nod the
> way, they nod the way!
> The hunt is up! I am the prey! The hunter's bow is
> strung!

Chapter VI

"BABY BANDITS"

*I*t was twenty-four hours before Detective Sergeant Flannagan awoke to the fact that something had been put over on him, and that a Kansas farmer's wife had done the putting.

He managed to piece it out finally from the narratives of the two tramps, and when he had returned to the Shorter home and listened to the contradictory and whole-souled improvisations of Shorter pere and mere he was convinced.

Whereupon he immediately telegraphed Chicago headquarters and obtained the necessary authority to proceed upon the trail of the fugitive, Byrne.

And so it was that Sergeant Flannagan landed in El Paso a few days later, drawn thither by various pieces of intelligence he had gathered en route, though with much delay and consequent vexation.

Even after he had quitted the train he was none too sure that he was upon the right trail though he at once repaired to a telegraph office and wired his chief that he was hot on the trail of the fugitive.

As a matter of fact he was much hotter than he imagined, for Billy and Bridge were that very minute not two squares from him, debating as to the future and the best manner of meeting it before it arrived.

"I think," said Billy, "that I'll duck across the border. I won't never be safe in little old U. S., an' with things hoppin' in Mexico the way they have been for the last few years I orter be able to lose myself pretty well.

"Now you're all right, ol' top. You don't have to duck nothin' for you ain't did nothin'. I don't know what you're runnin' away from; but I know it ain't nothin' the police is worryin' about — I can tell that by the way you act — so I guess we'll split here. You'd be a boob to cross if you don't have to, fer if Villa don't get you the Carranzistas will, unless the Zapatistas nab you first.

"Comin' or goin' some greasy-mugged highbinder's bound to croak you if you cross, from what little I've heard since we landed in El Paso.

"We'll feed up together tonight, fer the last time. Then I'll pull my freight." He was silent for a while, and then: "I hate to do it, bo, fer you're the whitest guy I ever struck," which was a great deal for Billy Byrne of Grand Avenue to say.

Bridge finished rolling a brown paper cigarette before he spoke.

"Your words are pure and unadulterated wisdom, my friend," he said. "The chances are scarcely even that two gringo hoboes would last the week out afoot and broke in Viva Mexico; but it has been many years since I followed the dictates of wisdom. Therefore I am going with you."

Billy grinned. He could not conceal his pleasure.

"You're past twenty-one," he said, "an' dry behind the ears. Let's go an' eat. There is still some of that twenty-five left."

Together they entered a saloon which Bridge remembered as permitting a very large consumption of free lunch upon the purchase of a single schooner of beer.

There were round tables scattered about the floor in front of the bar, and after purchasing their beer they carried it to one of these that stood in a far corner of the room close to a rear door.

Here Bridge sat on guard over the foaming open sesame to food while Billy crossed to the free lunch counter and appropriated all that a zealous attendant would permit him to carry off.

When he returned to the table he took a chair with his back to the wall in conformity to a habit of long standing when, as now, it had stood him in good stead to be in a position to see the other fellow at least as soon as the other fellow saw him. The other fellow being more often than not a large gentleman with a bit of shiny metal pinned to his left suspender strap.

"That guy's a tight one," said Billy, jerking his hand in the direction of the guardian of the free lunch. "I scoops up about a good, square meal for a canary bird, an' he makes me cough up half of it. Wants to know if I t'ink I can go into the restaurant business on a fi'-cent schooner of suds."

Bridge laughed.

"Well, you didn't do so badly at that," he said. "I know places where they'd indict you for grand larceny if you took much more than you have here."

"Rotten beer," commented Billy.

"Always is rotten down here," replied Bridge. "I sometimes think they put moth balls in it so it won't spoil."

Billy looked up and smiled. Then he raised his tall glass before him.

"Here's to," he started; but he got no further. His

eyes traveling past his companion fell upon the figure of a large man entering the low doorway.

At the same instant the gentleman's eyes fell upon Billy. Recognition lit those of each simultaneously. The big man started across the room on a run, straight toward Billy Byrne.

The latter leaped to his feet. Bridge, guessing what had happened, rose too.

"Flannagan!" he exclaimed.

The detective was tugging at his revolver, which had stuck in his hip pocket. Byrne reached for his own weapon. Bridge laid a hand on his arm.

"Not that, Billy!" he cried. "There's a door behind you. Here," and he pulled Billy backward toward the doorway in the wall behind them.

Byrne still clung to his schooner of beer, which he had transferred to his left hand as he sought to draw his gun. Flannagan was close to them. Bridge opened the door and strove to pull Billy through; but the latter hesitated just an instant, for he saw that it would be impossible to close and bar the door, provided it had a bar, before Flannagan would be against it with his great shoulders.

The policeman was still struggling to disentangle his revolver from the lining of his pocket. He was bellowing like a bull — yelling at Billy that he was under arrest. Men at the tables were on their feet. Those at the bar had turned around as Flannagan started to run across the floor. Now some of them were moving in the direction of the detective and his prey, but whether from curiosity or with sinister intentions it is difficult to say.

One thing, however, is certain — if all the love that was felt for policemen in general by the men in that room could have been combined in a single individual it still scarcely would have constituted a grand passion.

Flannagan felt rather than saw that others were closing in on him, and then, fortunately for himself, he thought, he managed to draw his weapon. It was just as Billy was fading through the doorway into the room beyond. He saw the revolver gleam in the policeman's hand and then it became evident why Billy had clung so tenaciously to his schooner of beer. Left-handed and hurriedly he threw it; but even Flannagan must have been constrained to admit that it was a good shot. It struck the detective directly in the midst of his features, gave him a nasty cut on the cheek as it broke and filled his eyes full of beer — and beer never was intended as an eye wash.

Spluttering and cursing, Flannagan came to a sudden stop, and when he had wiped the beer from his eyes he found that Billy Byrne had passed through the doorway and closed the door after him.

The room in which Billy and Bridge found themselves was a small one in the center of which was a large round table at which were gathered a half-dozen men at poker. Above the table swung a single arc lamp, casting a garish light upon the players beneath.

Billy looked quickly about for another exit, only to find that besides the doorway through which he had entered there was but a single aperture in the four walls-a small window, heavily barred. The place was a veritable trap.

At their hurried entrance the men had ceased their play, and one or two had risen in profane questioning and protest. Billy ignored them. He was standing with his shoulder against the door trying to secure it against the detective without; but there was neither bolt nor bar.

Flannagan hurtling against the opposite side exerted his noblest efforts to force an entrance to the room; but Billy Byrne's great weight held firm as Gibraltar.

His mind revolved various wild plans of escape; but none bade fair to offer the slightest foothold to hope.

The men at the table were clamoring for an explanation of the interruption. Two of them were approaching Billy with the avowed intention of "turning him out," when he turned his head suddenly toward them.

"Can de beef, you poor boobs," he cried. "Dere's a bunch o' dicks out dere — de joint's been pinched."

Instantly pandemonium ensued. Cards, chips, and money were swept as by magic from the board. A dozen dog-eared and filthy magazines and newspapers were snatched from a hiding place beneath the table, and in the fraction of a second the room was transformed from a gambling place to an innocent reading-room.

Billy grinned broadly. Flannagan had ceased his efforts to break down the door, and was endeavoring to persuade Billy that he might as well come out quietly and submit to arrest. Byrne had drawn his revolver again. Now he motioned to Bridge to come to his side.

"Follow me," he whispered. "Don't move 'til I move — then move sudden." Then, turning to the door again, "You big stiff," he cried, "you couldn't take a crip to a hospital, let alone takin' Billy Byrne to the still. Beat it, before I come out an' spread your beezer acrost your map."

If Billy had desired to arouse the ire of Detective Sergeant Flannagan by this little speech he succeeded quite as well as he could have hoped. Flannagan commenced to growl and threaten, and presently again hurled himself against the door.

Instantly Byrne wheeled and fired a single shot into the arc lamp, the shattered carbon rattled to the table with fragments of the globe, and Byrne stepped quickly to one side. The door flew open and Sergeant Flannagan dove headlong into the darkened room. A foot shot out from behind the opened door, and Flannagan, striking it, sprawled upon his face amidst the legs of the literary lights who held dog-eared magazines right-side up or upside down, as they chanced to have picked them up.

Simultaneously Billy Byrne and Bridge dodged through the open doorway, banged the door to behind them, and sped across the barroom toward the street.

As Flannagan shot into their midst the men at the table leaped to their feet and bolted for the doorway; but the detective was up and after them so quickly that only two succeeded in getting out of the room. One of these generously slammed the door in the faces of his fellows, and there they pulled and hauled at each other until Flannagan was among them.

In the pitch darkness he could recognize no one; but to be on the safe side he hit out promiscuously until he had driven them all from the door, then he stood with his back toward it — the inmates of the room his prisoners.

Thus he remained for a moment threatening to shoot at the first sound of movement in the room, and then he opened the door again, and stepping just outside ordered the prisoners to file out one at a time.

As each man passed him Flannagan scrutinized his face, and it was not until they had all emerged and he had reentered the room with a light that he discovered that once again his quarry had eluded him. Detective Sergeant Flannagan was peeved.

The sun smote down upon a dusty road. A heat-haze lay upon the arid land that stretched away upon either hand toward gray-brown hills. A little adobe hut, backed by a few squalid outbuildings, stood out, a screaming high-light in its coat of whitewash, against a background that was garish with light.

Two men plodded along the road. Their coats were off, the brims of their tattered hats were pulled down over eyes closed to mere slits against sun and dust

One of the men, glancing up at the distant hut, broke into verse:

> Yet then the sun was shining down, a-blazing on
> the little town,
> A mile or so 'way down the track a-dancing in the
> sun.
> But somehow, as I waited there, there came a
> shiver in the air,
> "The birds are flying south," he said. "The winter
> has begun."

His companion looked up at him who quoted.

"There ain't no track," he said, "an' that 'dobe shack don't look much like a town; but otherwise his Knibbs has got our number all right, all right. We are the birds a-flyin' south, and Flannagan was the shiver in the air. Flannagan is a reg'lar frost. Gee! but I betcha dat guy's sore."

"Why is it, Billy," asked Bridge, after a moment's silence, "that upon occasion you speak king's English after the manner of the boulevard, and again after that of the back alley? Sometimes you say 'that' and 'dat' in the same sentence. Your conversational clashes are numerous. Surely something or someone has cramped your original style."

"I was born and brought up on 'dat,'" explained Billy. "*She* taught me the other line of talk. Sometimes I forget. I had about twenty years of the other and only one of hers, and twenty to one is a long shot — more apt to lose than win."

"'She,' I take it, is *Penelope*," mused Bridge, half to himself. "She must have been a fine girl."

"'Fine' isn't the right word," Billy corrected him. "If a thing's fine there may be something finer, and then something else finest. She was better than finest. She — she was — why, Bridge, I'd have to be a walking dictionary to tell you what she was."

Bridge made no reply, and the two trudged on toward the whitewashed hut in silence for several minutes. Then Bridge broke it:

And you, my sweet Penelope, out there somewhere
          you wait for me
With buds of roses in your hair and kisses on your
          mouth.

Billy sighed and shook his head.

"There ain't no such luck for me," he said. "She's married to another gink now."

They came at last to the hut, upon the shady side of which they found a Mexican squatting puffing upon a cigarette, while upon the doorstep sat a woman, evidently his wife, busily engaged in the preparation of some manner of foodstuff contained in a large, shallow vessel. About them played a couple of half-naked children. A baby sprawled upon a blanket just within the doorway.

The man looked up, suspiciously, as the two approached. Bridge saluted him in fairly understandable Spanish, asking for food, and telling the man that they had money with which to pay for a little — not much, just a little.

The Mexican slowly unfolded himself and arose, motioning the strangers to follow him into the interior of the hut. The woman, at a word from her lord and master, followed them, and at his further dictation brought them frijoles and tortillas.

The price he asked was nominal; but his eyes never left Bridge's hands as the latter brought forth the money and handed it over. He appeared just a trifle disappointed when no more money than the stipulated purchase price was revealed to sight.

"Where you going?" he asked.

"We're looking for work," explained Bridge. "We want to get jobs on one of the American ranches or mines."

"You better go back," warned the Mexican. "I, myself, have nothing against the Americans, senor; but there are many of my countrymen who do not like you. The Americans are all leaving. Some already have been killed by bandits. It is not safe to go farther. Pesita's men are all about here. Even Mexicans are not safe from him. No one knows whether he is for Villa or Carranza. If he finds a Villa ranchero, then Pesita cries Viva Carranza! and his men kill and rob. If, on the other hand, a neighbor of the last victim hears of it in time, and later Pesita comes to him, he assures Pesita that he is for Carranza, whereupon Pesita cries Viva Villa! and falls upon the poor unfortunate, who is lucky if he escapes with his life. But Americans! Ah, Pesita asks them no questions. He hates them all, and kills them all, whenever he can lay his hands upon them. He has sworn to rid Mexico of the gringos."

"Wot's the Dago talkin' about?" asked Billy.

Bridge gave his companion a brief synopsis of the Mexican's conversation.

"Only the gentleman is not an Italian, Billy," he concluded. "He's a Mexican."

"Who said he was an Eyetalian?" demanded Byrne.

As the two Americans and the Mexican conversed within the hut there approached across the dusty flat, from the direction of the nearer hills, a party of five horsemen.

They rode rapidly, coming toward the hut from the side which had neither door nor window, so that those within had no warning of their coming. They were swarthy, ragged ruffians, fully armed, and with an equipment which suggested that they might be a part of a quasi-military organization.

Close behind the hut four of them dismounted while the fifth, remaining in his saddle, held the bridle reins of the horses of his companions. The latter crept stealthily around the outside of the building, toward the door — their carbines ready in their hands.

It was one of the little children who first discovered the presence of the newcomers. With a piercing scream she bolted into the interior and ran to cling to her mother's skirts.

Billy, Bridge, and the Mexican wheeled toward the doorway simultaneously to learn the cause of the girl's fright, and as they did so found themselves covered by four carbines in the hands of as many men.

As his eyes fell upon the faces of the intruders the countenance of the Mexican fell, while his wife dropped to the floor and embraced his knees, weeping.

"Wotinell?" ejaculated Billy Byrne. "What's doin'?"

"We seem to have been made prisoners," suggested Bridge; "but whether by Villistas or Carranzistas I do not know."

Their host understood his words and turned toward the two Americans.

"These are Pesita's men," he said.

"Yes," spoke up one of the bandits, "we are Pesita's men, and Pesita will be delighted, Miguel, to greet you, especially when he sees the sort of company you have been keeping. You know how much Pesita loves the gringos!"

"But this man does not even know us," spoke up Bridge. "We stopped here to get a meal. He never saw us before. We are on our way to the El Orobo Rancho in search of work. We have no money and have broken no laws. Let us go our way in peace. You can gain nothing by detaining us, and as for Miguel here — that is what you called him, I believe — I think from what he said to us that he loves a gringo about as much as your revered chief seems to."

Miguel looked his appreciation of Bridge's defense of him; but it was evident that he did not expect it to bear fruit. Nor did it. The brigand spokesman only grinned sardonically.

"You may tell all this to Pesita himself, senor," he said. "Now come — get a move on — beat it!" The fellow had once worked in El Paso and took great pride in his "higher English" education.

As he started to herd them from the hut Billy demurred. He turned toward Bridge.

"Most of this talk gets by me," he said. "I ain't jerry to all the Dago jabber yet, though I've copped off a little of it in the past two weeks. Put me wise to the gink's lay."

"Elementary, Watson, elementary," replied Bridge. "We are captured by bandits, and they are going to take us to their delightful chief who will doubtless have us shot at sunrise."

"Bandits?" snapped Billy, with a sneer. "Youse don't call dese little runts bandits?"

"Baby bandits, Billy, baby bandits," replied Bridge.

"An' you're goin' to stan' fer lettin' 'em pull off this rough stuff without handin' 'em a come-back?" demanded Byrne.

"We seem to be up against just that very thing," said Bridge. "There are four carbines quite ready for us. It would mean sudden death to resist now. Later we may find an opportunity — I think we'd better act simple and wait." He spoke in a quick, low whisper, for the spokesman of the brigands evidently understood a little English and was on the alert for any trickery.

Billy shrugged, and when their captors again urged

them forward he went quietly; but the expression on his face might have perturbed the Mexicans had they known Billy Byrne of Grand Avenue better — he was smiling happily.

Miguel had two ponies in his corral. These the brigands appropriated, placing Billy upon one and Miguel and Bridge upon the other. Billy's great weight rendered it inadvisable to double him up with another rider.

As they were mounting Billy leaned toward Bridge and whispered:

"I'll get these guys, pal — watch me," he said.

"I am with thee, William! — horse, foot, and artillery," laughed Bridge.

"Which reminds me," said Billy, "that I have an ace-in-the-hole — the boobs never frisked me."

"And I am reminded," returned Bridge, as the horses started off to the yank of hackamore ropes in the hands of the brigands who were leading them, "of a touching little thing of Service's:

Just think! Some night the stars will gleam
    Upon a cold gray stone,
And trace a name with silver beam,
    And lo! 'twill be your own.

"You're a cheerful guy," was Billy's only comment.

Chapter VII

IN PESITA'S CAMP

*P*esita was a short, stocky man with a large, dark mustache. He attired himself after his own ideas of what should constitute the uniform of a general — ideas more or less influenced and modified by the chance and caprice of fortune.

At the moment that Billy, Bridge, and Miguel were dragged into his presence his torso was enwrapped in a once resplendent coat covered with yards of gold braid. Upon his shoulders were brass epaulets such as are connected only in one's mind with the ancient chorus ladies of the light operas of fifteen or twenty years ago. Upon his legs were some rusty and ragged overalls. His feet were bare.

He scowled ferociously at the prisoners while his lieutenant narrated the thrilling facts of their capture — thrilling by embellishment.

"You are Americanos?" he asked of Bridge and Billy.

Both agreed that they were. Then Pesita turned toward Miguel.

"Where is Villa?" he asked.

"How should I know, my general?" parried Miguel. "Who am I — a poor man with a tiny rancho — to know of the movements of the great ones of the earth? I did not even know where was the great General Pesita until now I am brought into his gracious presence, to throw myself at his feet and implore that I be permitted to serve him in even the meanest of capacities."

Pesita appeared not to hear what Miguel had said. He turned his shoulder toward the man, and addressed Billy in broken English.

"You were on your way to El Orobo Rancho, eh? Are you acquainted there?" he asked.

Billy replied that they were not — merely looking for employment upon an American-owned ranch or in an American mine.

"Why did you leave your own country?" asked Pesita. "What do you want here in Mexico?"

"Well, ol' top," replied Billy, "you see de birds was flyin' south an' winter was in de air, an a fat-head dick from Chi was on me trail — so I ducks."

"Ducks?" queried Pesita, mystified. "Ah, the ducks — they fly south, I see."

"Naw, you poor simp — I blows," explained Billy.

"Ah, yes," agreed Pesita, not wishing to admit any ignorance of plain American even before a despised gringo. "But the large-faced dick — what might that be? I have spend much time in the States, but I do not know that"

"I said 'fat-head dick' — dat's a fly cop," Billy elucidated.

"It is he then that is the bird." Pesita beamed at this evidence of his own sagacity. "He fly."

"Flannagan ain't no bird — Flannagan's a dub."

Bridge came to the rescue.

"My erudite friend means," he explained, "that the

police chased him out of the United States of America."

Pesita raised his eyebrows. All was now clear to him.

"But why did he not say so?" he asked.

"He tried to," said Bridge. "He did his best."

"Quit yer kiddin'," admonished Billy.

A bright fight suddenly burst upon Pesita. He turned upon Bridge.

"Your friend is not then an American?" he asked. "I guessed it. That is why I could not understand him. He speaks the language of the gringo less well even than I. From what country is he?"

Billy Byrne would have asserted with some show of asperity that he was nothing if not American; but Bridge was quick to see a possible loophole for escape for his friend in Pesita's belief that Billy was no gringo, and warned the latter to silence by a quick motion of his head.

"He's from 'Gran' Avenoo,'" he said. "It is not exactly in Germany; but there are a great many Germans there. My friend is a native, so he don't speak German or English either — they have a language of their own in 'Gran' Avenoo'."

"I see," said Pesita — "a German colony. I like the Germans — they furnish me with much ammunition and rifles. They are my very good friends. Take Miguel and the gringo away" — this to the soldiers who had brought the prisoners to him — "I will speak further with this man from Granavenoo."

When the others had passed out of hearing Pesita addressed Billy.

"I am sorry, senor," he said, "that you have been put to so much inconvenience. My men could not know that you were not a gringo; but I can make it all right. I will make it all right. You are a big man. The gringos have chased you from their country as they chased me.

I hate them. You hate them. But enough of them. You have no business in Mexico except to seek work. I give you work. You are big. You are strong. You are like a bull. You stay with me, senor, and I make you captain. I need men what can talk some English and look like gringo. You do fine. We make much money — you and I. We make it all time while we fight to liberate my poor Mexico. When Mexico liberate we fight some more to liberate her again. The Germans they give me much money to liberate Mexico, and — there are other ways of getting much money when one is riding around through rich country with soldiers liberating his poor, bleeding country. Sabe?"

"Yep, I guess I savvy," said Billy, "an' it listens all right to me's far's you've gone. My pal in on it?"

"Eh?"

"You make my frien' a captain, too?"

Pesita held up his hands and rolled his eyes in holy horror. Take a gringo into his band? It was unthinkable.

"He shot," he cried. "I swear to kill all gringo. I become savior of my country. I rid her of all Americanos."

"Nix on the captain stuff fer me, then," said Billy, firmly. "That guy's a right one. If any big stiff thinks he can croak little ol' Bridge while Billy Byrne's aroun' he's got anudder t'ink comin'. Why, me an' him's just like brudders."

"You like this gringo?" asked Pesita.

"You bet," cried Billy.

Pesita thought for several minutes. In his mind was a scheme which required the help of just such an individual as this stranger — someone who was utterly unknown in the surrounding country and whose presence in a town could not by any stretch of the imagination be connected in any way with the bandit, Pesita.

"I tell you," he said. "I let your friend go. I send him under safe escort to El Orobo Rancho. Maybe he help us there after a while. If you stay I let him go. Otherwise I shoot you both with Miguel."

"Wot you got it in for Mig fer?" asked Billy. "He's a harmless sort o' guy."

"He Villista. Villista with gringos run Mexico — gringos and the church. Just like Huerta would have done it if they'd given him a chance, only Huerta more for church than for gringos."

"Aw, let the poor boob go," urged Billy, "an' I'll come along wit you. Why he's got a wife an' kids — you wouldn't want to leave them without no one to look after them in this God-forsaken country!"

Pesita grinned indulgently.

"Very well, Senor Captain," he said, bowing low. "I let Miguel and your honorable friend go. I send safe escort with them."

"Bully fer you, ol' pot!" exclaimed Billy, and Pesita smiled delightedly in the belief that some complimentary title had been applied to him in the language of "Granavenoo." "I'll go an' tell 'em," said Billy.

"Yes," said Pesita, "and say to them that they will start early in the morning."

As Billy turned and walked in the direction that the soldiers had led Bridge and Miguel, Pesita beckoned to a soldier who leaned upon his gun at a short distance from his "general" — a barefooted, slovenly attempt at a headquarters orderly.

"Send Captain Rozales to me," directed Pesita.

The soldier shuffled away to where a little circle of men in wide-brimmed, metal-encrusted hats squatted in the shade of a tree, chatting, laughing, and rolling cigarettes. He saluted one of these and delivered his message, whereupon the tall, gaunt Captain Rozales arose and came over to Pesita.

"The big one who was brought in today is not a gringo," said Pesita, by way of opening the conversation. "He is from Granavenoo. He can be of great service to us, for he is very friendly with the Germans — yet he looks like a gringo and could pass for one. We can utilize him. Also he is very large and appears to be equally strong. He should make a good fighter and we have none too many. I have made him a captain."

Rozales grinned. Already among Pesita's following of a hundred men there were fifteen captains.

"Where is Granavenoo?" asked Rozales.

"You mean to say, my dear captain," exclaimed Pesita, "that a man of your education does not know where Granavenoo is? I am surprised. Why, it is a German colony."

"Yes, of course. I recall it well now. For the moment it had slipped my mind. My grandfather who was a great traveler was there many times. I have heard him speak of it often."

"But I did not summon you that we might discuss European geography," interrupted Pesita. "I sent for you to tell you that the stranger would not consent to serve me unless I liberated his friend, the gringo, and that sneaking spy of a Miguel. I was forced to yield, for we can use the stranger. So I have promised, my dear captain, that I shall send them upon their road with a safe escort in the morning, and you shall command the guard. Upon your life respect my promise, Rozales; but if some of Villa's cutthroats should fall upon you, and in the battle, while you were trying to defend the gringo and Miguel, both should be slain by the bullets of the Villistas — ah, but it would be deplorable, Rozales, but it would not be your fault. Who, indeed, could blame you who had fought well and risked your men and yourself in the performance of your sacred duty? Rozales, should such a thing occur what could I do in token of my great pleasure other than make you a colonel?"

"I shall defend them with my life, my general," cried Rozales, bowing low.

"Good!" cried Pesita. "That is all."

Rozales started back toward the ring of smokers.

"Ah, Captain!" cried Pesita. "Another thing. Will you make it known to the other officers that the stranger from Granavenoo is a captain and that it is my wish that he be well treated, but not told so much as might injure him, or his usefulness, about our sacred work of liberating poor, bleeding unhappy Mexico."

Again Rozales bowed and departed. This time he was not recalled.

Billy found Bridge and Miguel squatting on the ground with two dirty-faced peons standing guard over them. The latter were some little distance away. They made no objection when Billy approached the prisoners though they had looked in mild surprise when they saw him crossing toward them without a guard.

Billy sat down beside Bridge, and broke into a laugh.

"What's the joke?" asked Bridge. "Are we going to be hanged instead of being shot?"

"We ain't goin' to be either," said Billy, "an' I'm a captain. Whaddaya know about that?"

He explained all that had taken place between himself and Pesita while Bridge and Miguel listened attentively to his every word.

"I t'ought it was about de only way out fer us," said Billy. "We were in worse than I t'ought."

"Can the Bowery stuff, Billy," cried Bridge, "and talk like a white man. You can, you know."

"All right, bo," cried Billy, good-naturedly. "You see I forget when there is anything pressing like this, to chew about. Then I fall back into the old lingo. Well, as I was saying, I didn't want to do it unless you would stay too, but he wouldn't have you. He has it in for all gringos, and that bull you passed him about me being from a foreign country called Grand Avenue! He fell for it like a rube for the tapped-wire stuff. He said if I wouldn't stay and help him he'd croak the bunch of us."

"How about that ace-in-the-hole, you were telling me about?" asked Bridge.

"I still got it," and Billy fondled something hard that swung under his left arm beneath his shirt; "but, Lord, man! what could I do against the whole bunch? I might get a few of them; but they'd get us all in the end. This other way is better, though I hate to have to split with you, old man."

He was silent then for a moment, looking hard at the ground. Bridge whistled, and cleared his throat.

"I've always wanted to spend a year in Rio," he said. "We'll meet there, when you can make your get-away."

"You've said it," agreed Byrne. "It's Rio as soon as we can make it. Pesita's promised to set you both loose in the morning and send you under safe escort — Miguel to his happy home, and you to El Orobo Rancho. I guess the old stiff isn't so bad after all."

Miguel had pricked up his ears at the sound of the word *escort*. He leaned far forward, closer to the two Americans, and whispered.

"Who is to command the escort?" he asked.

"I dunno," said Billy. "What difference does it make?"

"It makes all the difference between life and death for your friend and for me," said Miguel. "There is no reason why I should need an escort. I know my way throughout all Chihuahua as well as Pesita or any of his cutthroats. I have come and gone all my life without an escort. Of course your friend is different. It might be well for him to have company to El Orobo. Maybe it is all right; but wait until we learn who commands the escort. I know Pesita well. I know his methods. If Rozales rides out with us tomorrow morning you may say good-bye to your friend forever, for you will never see him in Rio, or elsewhere. He and I will be dead before ten o'clock."

"What makes you think that, bo?" demanded Billy.

"I do not think, senor," replied Miguel; "I know."

"Well," said Billy, "we'll wait and see."

"If it is Rozales, say nothing," said Miguel. "It will do no good; but we may then be on the watch, and if possible you might find the means to obtain a couple of revolvers for us. In which case —" he shrugged and permitted a faint smile to flex his lips.

As they talked a soldier came and announced that they were no longer prisoners — they were to have the freedom of the camp; "but," he concluded, "the general requests that you do not pass beyond the limits of the camp. There are many desperadoes in the hills and he fears for your safety, now that you are his guests."

The man spoke Spanish, so that it was necessary that Bridge interpret his words for the benefit of Billy, who had understood only part of what he said.

"Ask him," said Byrne, "if that stuff goes for me, too."

"He says no," replied Bridge after questioning the soldier, "that the captain is now one of them, and may go and come as do the other officers. Such are Pesita's orders."

Billy arose. The messenger had returned to his post at headquarters. The guard had withdrawn, leaving the three men alone.

"So long, old man," said Billy. "If I'm goin' to be of any help to you and Mig the less I'm seen with you the better. I'll blow over and mix with the Dago bunch, an' practice sittin' on my heels. It seems to be the right

dope down here, an' I got to learn all I can about bein'
a greaser seein' that I've turned one."

"Good-bye Billy, remember Rio," said Bridge.

"And the revolvers, senor," added Miguel.

"You bet," replied Billy, and strolled off in the direction of the little circle of cigarette smokers.

As he approached them Rozales looked up and
smiled. Then, rising, extended his hand.

"Senor Captain," he said, "we welcome you. I am
Captain Rozales." He hesitated waiting for Billy to give
his name.

"My monacker's Byrne," said Billy. "Pleased to meet
you, Cap."

"Ah, Captain Byrne," and Rozales proceeded to in-
troduce the newcomer to his fellow-officers.

Several, like Rozales, were educated men who had
been officers in the army under former regimes, but
had turned bandit as the safer alternative to suffering
immediate death at the hands of the faction then in
power. The others, for the most part, were pure-
blooded Indians whose adult lives had been spent in
outlawry and brigandage. All were small of stature
beside the giant, Byrne. Rozales and two others spoke
English. With those Billy conversed. He tried to learn
from them the name of the officer who was to command the escort that was to accompany Bridge and
Miguel into the valley on the morrow; but Rozales and
the others assured him that they did not know.

When he had asked the question Billy had been
looking straight at Rozales, and he had seen the man's
pupils contract and noticed the slight backward movement of the body which also denotes determination.
Billy knew, therefore, that Rozales was lying. He did
know who was to command the escort, and there was
something sinister in that knowledge or the fellow
would not have denied it.

The American began to consider plans for saving his friend from the fate which Pesita had outlined for him. Rozales, too, was thinking rapidly. He was no fool. Why had the stranger desired to know who was to command the escort? He knew none of the officers personally. What difference then, did it make to him who rode out on the morrow with his friend? Ah, but Miguel knew that it would make a difference. Miguel had spoken to the new captain, and aroused his suspicions.

Rozales excused himself and rose. A moment later he was in conversation with Pesita, unburdening himself of his suspicions, and outlining a plan.

"Do not send me in charge of the escort," he advised. "Send Captain Byrne himself."

Pesita pooh-poohed the idea.

"But wait," urged Rozales. "Let the stranger ride in command, with a half-dozen picked men who will see that nothing goes wrong. An hour before dawn I will send two men — they will be our best shots — on ahead. They will stop at a place we both know, and about noon the Captain Byrne and his escort will ride back to camp and tell us that they were attacked by a troop of Villa's men, and that both our guests were killed. It will be sad; but it will not be our fault. We will swear vengeance upon Villa, and the Captain Byrne will hate him as a good Pesitista should."

"You have the cunning of the Coyote, my captain," cried Pesita. "It shall be done as you suggest. Go now, and I will send for Captain Byrne, and give him his orders for the morning."

As Rozales strolled away a figure rose from the shadows at the side of Pesita's tent and slunk off into the darkness.

Chapter VIII

BILLY'S FIRST COMMAND

*A*nd so it was that having breakfasted in the morning Bridge and Miguel started downward toward the valley protected by an escort under Captain Billy Byrne. An old service jacket and a wide-brimmed hat, both donated by brother officers, constituted Captain Byrne's uniform. His mount was the largest that the picket line of Pesita's forces could produce. Billy loomed large amongst his men.

For an hour they rode along the trail, Billy and Bridge conversing upon various subjects, none of which touched upon the one uppermost in the mind of each. Miguel rode, silent and preoccupied. The evening before he had whispered something to Bridge as he had crawled out of the darkness to lie close to the American, and during a brief moment that morning Bridge had found an opportunity to relay the Mexican's message to Billy Byrne.

The latter had but raised his eyebrows a trifle at the time, but later he smiled more than was usual with him. Something seemed to please him immensely.

Beside him at the head of the column rode Bridge and Miguel. Behind them trailed the six swarthy little troopers — the picked men upon whom Pesita could depend.

They had reached a point where the trail passes through a narrow dry arroyo which the waters of the rainy season had cut deep into the soft, powdery soil. Upon either bank grew cacti and mesquite, forming a sheltering screen behind which a regiment might have hidden. The place was ideal for an ambuscade.

"Here, Senor Capitan," whispered Miguel, as they neared the entrance to the trap.

A low hill shut off from their view all but the head of the cut, and it also hid them from the sight of any possible enemy which might have been lurking in wait for them farther down the arroyo.

At Miguel's words Byrne wheeled his horse to the right away from the trail which led through the bottom of the waterway and around the base of the hill, or rather in that direction, for he had scarce deviated from the direct way before one of the troopers spurred to his side, calling out in Spanish that he was upon the wrong trail.

"Wot's this guy chewin' about?" asked Billy, turning to Miguel.

"He says you must keep to the arroyo, Senor Capitan," explained the Mexican.

"Tell him to go back into his stall," was Byrne's laconic rejoinder, as he pushed his mount forward to pass the brigand.

The soldier was voluble in his objections. Again he reined in front of Billy, and by this time his five fellows had spurred forward to block the way.

"This is the wrong trail," they cried. "Come this other way, Capitan. Pesita has so ordered it."

Catching the drift of their remarks, Billy waved them to one side.

"I'm bossin' this picnic," he announced. "Get out o' the way, an' be quick about it if you don't want to be hurted."

Again he rode forward. Again the troopers interposed their mounts, and this time their leader cocked his carbine. His attitude was menacing. Billy was close to him. Their ponies were shoulder to shoulder, that of the bandit almost broadside of the trail.

Now Billy Byrne was more than passing well acquainted with many of the fundamental principles of sudden brawls. it is safe to say that he had never heard of Van Bibber; but he knew, as well as Van Bibber knew, that it is well to hit first.

Without a word and without warning he struck, leaning forward with all the weight of his body behind his blow, and catching the man full beneath the chin he lifted him as neatly from his saddle as though a battering ram had struck him.

Simultaneously Bridge and Miguel drew revolvers from their shirts and as Billy wheeled his pony toward the remaining five they opened fire upon them.

The battle was short and sweet. One almost escaped but Miguel, who proved to be an excellent revolver shot, brought him down at a hundred yards. He then, with utter disregard for the rules of civilized warfare, dispatched those who were not already dead.

"We must let none return to carry false tales to Pesita," he explained.

Even Billy Byrne winced at the ruthlessness of the cold-blooded murders; but he realized the necessity which confronted them though he could not have brought himself to do the things which the Mexican did with such sang-froid and even evident enjoyment.

"Now for the others!" cried Miguel, when he had

assured himself that each of the six were really quite dead.

Spurring after him Billy and Bridge ran their horses over the rough ground at the base of the little hill, and then parallel to the arroyo for a matter of a hundred yards, where they espied two Indians, carbines in hand, standing in evident consternation because of the un-expected fusillade of shots which they had just heard and which they were unable to account for.

At the sight of the three the sharpshooters dropped behind cover and fired. Billy's horse stumbled at the first report, caught himself, reared high upon his hind legs and then toppled over, dead.

His rider, throwing himself to one side, scrambled to his feet and fired twice at the partially concealed men. Miguel and Bridge rode in rapidly to close quar-ters, firing as they came. One of the two men Pesita had sent to assassinate his "guests" dropped his gun, clutched at his breast, screamed, and sank back behind a clump of mesquite. The other turned and leaped over the edge of the bank into the arroyo, rolling and tumbling to the bottom in a cloud of dry dust.

As he rose to his feet and started on a run up the bed of the dry stream, dodging a zigzag course from one bit of scant cover to another Billy Byrne stepped to the edge of the washout and threw his carbine to his shoulder. His face was flushed, his eyes sparkled, a smile lighted his regular features.

"This is the life!" he cried, and pulled the trigger.

The man beneath him, running for his life like a frightened jackrabbit, sprawled forward upon his face, made a single effort to rise and then slumped limply down, forever.

Miguel and Bridge, dismounted now, came to Byrne's side. The Mexican was grinning broadly.

"The captain is one grand fighter," he said. "How

my dear general would admire such a man as the captain. Doubtless he would make him a colonel. Come with me Senor Capitan and your fortune is made."

"Come where?" asked Billy Byrne.

"To the camp of the liberator of poor, bleeding Mexico — to General Francisco Villa."

"Nothin' doin'," said Billy. "I'm hooked up with this Pesita person now, an' I guess I'll stick. He's given me more of a run for my money in the last twenty-four hours than I've had since I parted from my dear old friend, the Lord of Yoka."

"But Senor Capitan," cried Miguel, "you do not mean to say that you are going back to Pesita! He will shoot you down with his own hand when he has learned what has happened here."

"I guess not," said Billy.

"You'd better go with Miguel, Billy," urged Bridge. "Pesita will not forgive you this. You've cost him eight men today and he hasn't any more men than he needs at best. Besides you've made a monkey of him and unless I miss my guess you'll have to pay for it."

"No," said Billy, "I kind o' like this Pesita gent. I think I'll stick around with him for a while yet. Anyhow until I've had a chance to see his face after I've made my report to him. You guys run along now and make your get-away good, an' I'll beat it back to camp."

He crossed to where the two horses of the slain marksmen were hidden, turned one of them loose and mounted the other.

"So long, boes!" he cried, and with a wave of his hand wheeled about and spurred back along the trail over which they had just come.

Miguel and Bridge watched him for a moment, then they, too, mounted and turned away in the opposite direction. Bridge recited no verse for the balance of that day. His heart lay heavy in his bosom, for he missed Billy Byrne, and was fearful of the fate which awaited him at the camp of the bandit.

Billy, blithe as a lark, rode gaily back along the trail to camp. He looked forward with unmixed delight to his coming interview with Pesita, and to the wild, half-savage life which association with the bandit promised. All his life had Billy Byrne fed upon excitement and adventure. As gangster, thug, holdup man and second-story artist Billy had found food for his appetite within the dismal, sooty streets of Chicago's great West Side, and then Fate had flung him upon the savage shore of Yoka to find other forms of adventure where the best that is in a strong man may be brought out in the stern battle for existence against primeval men and conditions. The West Side had developed only Billy's basest characteristics. He might have slipped back easily into the old ways had it not been for *her* and the recollection of that which he had read in her eyes. Love had been there; but greater than that to hold a man into the straight and narrow path of decency and honor had been respect and admiration. It had seemed incredible to Billy that a goddess should feel such things for him — for the same man her scornful lips once had branded as coward and mucker; yet he had read the truth aright, and since then Billy Byrne had done his best according to the fight that had been given him to deserve the belief she had in him.

So far there had crept into his consciousness no disquieting doubts as to the consistency of his recent action in joining the force of a depredating Mexican outlaw. Billy knew nothing of the political conditions of the republic. Had Pesita told him that he was president of Mexico, Billy could not have disputed the statement from any knowledge of facts which he possessed. As a matter of fact about all Billy had ever known of Mexico was that it had some connection with an important place called Juarez where running meets were held.

To Billy Byrne, then, Pesita was a real general, and Billy, himself, a bona fide captain. He had entered an army which was at war with some other army. What they were warring about Billy knew not, nor did he care. There should be fighting and he loved that — that much he knew. The ethics of Pesita's warfare troubled him not. He had heard that some great American general had said: "War is hell." Billy was willing to take his word for it, and accept anything which came in the guise of war as entirely proper and as it should be.

The afternoon was far gone when Billy drew rein in the camp of the outlaw band. Pesita with the bulk of his raiders was out upon some excursion to the north. Only half a dozen men lolled about, smoking or sleeping away the hot day. They looked at Billy in evident surprise when they saw him riding in alone; but they asked no questions and Billy offered no explanation — his report was for the ears of Pesita only.

The balance of the day Billy spent in acquiring further knowledge of Spanish by conversing with those of the men who remained awake, and asking innumerable questions. It was almost sundown when Pesita rode in. Two riderless horses were led by troopers in the rear of the little column and three men swayed painfully in their saddles and their clothing was stained with blood.

Evidently Pesita had met with resistance. There was much voluble chattering on the part of those who had remained behind in their endeavors to extract from their returning comrades the details of the day's enterprise. By piecing together the various scraps of conversation he could understand Billy discovered that Pesita had ridden far to demand tribute from a wealthy ranchero, only to find that word of his coming had preceded him and brought a large detachment of Villa's regulars who concealed themselves about the house and outbuildings until Pesita and his entire force were well within close range.

"We were lucky to get off as well as we did," said an officer.

Billy grinned inwardly as he thought of the pleasant frame of mind in which Pesita might now be expected to receive the news that eight of his troopers had been killed and his two "guests" safely removed from the sphere of his hospitality.

And even as his mind dwelt delightedly upon the subject a ragged Indian carrying a carbine and with heavy silver spurs strapped to his bare feet approached and saluted him.

"General Pesita wishes Senor Capitan Byrne to report to him at once," said the man.

"Sure Mike!" replied Billy, and made his way through the pandemonium of the camp toward the headquarters tent.

As he went he slipped his hand inside his shirt and loosened something which hung beneath his left arm.

"Li'l ol' ace-in-the-hole," he murmured affectionately.

He found Pesita pacing back and forth before his tent — an energetic bundle of nerves which no amount of hard riding and fighting could tire or discourage.

As Billy approached Pesita shot a quick glance at his face, that he might read, perhaps, in his new officer's expression whether anger or suspicion had been aroused by the killing of his American friend, for Pesita never dreamed but that Bridge had been dead since mid-forenoon.

"Well," said Pesita, smiling, "you left Senor Bridge and Miguel safely at their destination?"

"I couldn't take 'em all the way," replied Billy, "cause I didn't have no more men to guard 'em with; but I seen 'em past the danger I guess an' well on their way."

"You had no men?" questioned Pesita. "You had six troopers."

"Oh, they was all croaked before we'd been gone two hours. You see it happens like this: We got as far as that dry arroyo just before the trail drops down into the valley, when up jumps a bunch of this here Villa's guys and commenced takin' pot shots at us.

"Seein' as how I was sent to guard Bridge an' Mig, I makes them dismount and hunt cover, and then me an' my men wades in and cleans up the bunch. They was only a few of them but they croaked the whole bloomin' six o' mine.

"I tell you it was some scrap while it lasted; but I saved your guests from gettin' hurted an' I know that that's what you sent me to do. It's too bad about the six men we lost but, leave it to me, we'll get even with that Villa guy yet. Just lead me to 'im."

As he spoke Billy commenced scratching himself beneath the left arm, and then, as though to better reach the point of irritation, he slipped his hand inside his shirt. If Pesita noticed the apparently innocent little act, or interpreted it correctly may or may not have been the fact. He stood looking straight into Byrne's eyes for a full minute. His face denoted neither baffled rage nor contemplated revenge. Presently a slow smile raised his heavy mustache and revealed his strong, white teeth.

"You have done well, Captain Byrne," he said. "You are a man after my own heart," and he extended his hand.

A half-hour later Billy walked slowly back to his own blankets, and to say that he was puzzled would scarce have described his mental state.

"I can't quite make that gink out," he mused. "Either he's a mighty good loser or else he's a deep one who'll wait a year to get me the way he wants to get me."

And Pesita a few moments later was saying to Captain Rozales:

"I should have shot him if I could spare such a man; but it is seldom I find one with the courage and effrontery he possesses. Why think of it, Rozales, he kills eight of my men, and lets my prisoners escape, and then dares to come back and tell me about it when he might easily have gotten away. Villa would have made him an officer for this thing, and Miguel must have told him so. He found out in some way about your little plan and he turned the tables on us. We can use him, Rozales, but we must watch him. Also, my dear captain, watch his right hand and when he slips it into his shirt be careful that you do not draw on him – unless you happen to be behind him."

Rozales was not inclined to take his chief's view of Byrne's value to them. He argued that the man was guilty of disloyalty and therefore a menace. What he thought, but did not advance as an argument, was of a different nature. Rozales was filled with rage to think that the newcomer had outwitted him, and beaten him at his own game, and he was jealous, too, of the man's ascendancy in the esteem of Pesita; but he hid his personal feelings beneath a cloak of seeming acquiescence in his chief's views, knowing that some day his time would come when he might rid himself of the danger of this obnoxious rival.

"And tomorrow," continued Pesita, "I am sending him to Cuivaca. Villa has considerable funds in bank there, and this stranger can learn what I want to know about the size of the detachment holding the town, and the habits of the garrison."

Chapter IX

BARBARA IN MEXICO

*T*he manager of El Orobo Rancho was an American named Grayson. He was a tall, wiry man whose education had been acquired principally in the cow camps of Texas, where, among other things one does *not* learn to love nor trust a greaser. As a result of this early training Grayson was peculiarly unfitted in some respects to manage an American ranch in Mexico; but he was a just man, and so if his vaqueros did not love him, they at least respected him, and everyone who was or possessed the latent characteristics of a wrongdoer feared him.

Perhaps it is not fair to say that Grayson was in any way unfitted for the position he held, since as a matter of fact he was an ideal ranch foreman, and, if the truth be known, the simple fact that he was a gringo would have been sufficient to have won him the hatred of the Mexicans who worked under him — not in the course of their everyday relations; but when the fires of racial animosity were fanned to flame by some untoward incident upon either side of the border.

Today Grayson was particularly rabid. The more so because he could not vent his anger upon the cause of it, who was no less a person than his boss.

It seemed incredible to Grayson that any man of intelligence could have conceived and then carried out the fool thing which the boss had just done, which was to have come from the safety of New York City to the hazards of warring Mexico, bringing — and this was the worst feature of it — his daughter with him. And at such a time! Scarce a day passed without its rumors or reports of new affronts and even atrocities being perpetrated upon American residents of Mexico. Each day, too, the gravity of these acts increased. From mere insult they had run of late to assault and even to murder. Nor was the end in sight.

Pesita had openly sworn to rid Mexico of the gringo — to kill on sight every American who fell into his hands. And what could Grayson do in case of a determined attack upon the rancho? It is true he had a hundred men — laborers and vaqueros, but scarce a dozen of these were Americans, and the rest would, almost without exception, follow the inclinations of consanguinity in case of trouble.

To add to Grayson's irritability he had just lost his bookkeeper, and if there was one thing more than any other that Grayson hated it was pen and ink. The youth had been a "lunger" from Iowa, a fairly nice little chap, and entirely suited to his duties under any other circumstances than those which prevailed in Mexico at that time. He was in mortal terror of his life every moment that he was awake, and at last had given in to the urge of cowardice and resigned. The day previous he had been bundled into a buckboard and driven over to the Mexican Central which, at that time, still was operating trains — occasionally — between Chihuahua and Juarez.

His mind filled with these unpleasant thoughts, Grayson sat at his desk in the office of the ranch trying to unravel the riddle of a balance sheet which would not balance. Mixed with the blue of the smoke from his briar was the deeper azure of a spirited monologue in which Grayson was engaged.

A girl was passing the building at the moment. At her side walked a gray-haired man — one of those men whom you just naturally fit into a mental picture of a director's meeting somewhere along Wall Street.

"Sich langwidge!" cried the girl, with a laugh, covering her ears with her palms.

The man at her side smiled.

"I can't say that I blame him much, Barbara," he replied. "It was a very foolish thing for me to bring you down here at this time. I can't understand what ever possessed me to do it."

"Don't blame yourself, dear," remonstrated the girl, "when it was all my fault. I begged and begged and begged until you had to consent, and I'm not sorry either — if nothing happens to you because of our coming. I couldn't stay in New York another minute. Everyone was so snoopy, and I could just tell that they were dying to ask questions about Billy and me."

"I can't get it through my head yet, Barbara," said the man, "why in the world you broke with Billy Mallory. He's one of the finest young men in New York City today — just my ideal of the sort of man I'd like my only daughter to marry."

"I tried, Papa," said the girl in a low voice; "but I couldn't — I just couldn't."

"Was it because —" the man stopped abruptly. "Well, never mind dear, I shan't be snoopy too. Here now, you run along and do some snooping yourself about the ranch. I want to stop in and have a talk with

Grayson."

Down by one of the corrals where three men were busily engaged in attempting to persuade an unbroken pony that a spade bit is a pleasant thing to wear in one's mouth, Barbara found a seat upon a wagon box which commanded an excellent view of the entertainment going on within the corral. As she sat there experiencing a combination of admiration for the agility and courage of the men and pity for the horse the tones of a pleasant masculine voice broke in upon her thoughts.

"Out there somewhere!" says I to me. "By Gosh, I
       guess, thats poetry!
"Out there somewhere — Penelope — with kisses on
       her mouth!"
And then, thinks I, "O college guy! your talk it
       gets me in the eye,
The north is creeping in the air, the birds are flying
       south."

Barbara swung around to view the poet. She saw a slender man astride a fagged Mexican pony. A ragged coat and ragged trousers covered the man's nakedness. Indian moccasins protected his feet, while a torn and shapeless felt hat sat upon his well-shaped head. *American* was written all over him. No one could have imagined him anything else. Apparently he was a tramp as well — his apparel proclaimed him that; but there were two discordant notes in the otherwise harmonious ensemble of your typical bo. He was clean shaven and he rode a pony. He rode erect, too, with the easy seat of an army officer.

At sight of the girl he raised his battered hat and swept it low to his pony's shoulder as he bent in a profound bow.

"I seek the majordomo, senorita," he said.

"Mr. Grayson is up at the office, that little building to the left of the ranchhouse," replied the girl, pointing.

The newcomer had addressed her in Spanish, and as he heard her reply, in pure and liquid English, his eyes widened a trifle; but the familiar smile with which he had greeted her left his face, and his parting bow was much more dignified though no less profound than its predecessor.

And you, my sweet Penelope, out there somewhere
        you wait for me,
With buds of roses in your hair and kisses on your
        mouth.

Grayson and his employer both looked up as the words of Knibbs' poem floated in to them through the open window.

"I wonder where that blew in from," remarked Grayson, as his eyes discovered Bridge astride the tired pony, looking at him through the window. A polite smile touched the stranger's lips as his eyes met Grayson's, and then wandered past him to the imposing figure of the Easterner.

"Good evening, gentlemen," said Bridge.

"Evenin'," snapped Grayson. "Go over to the cookhouse and the Chink'll give you something to eat. Turn your pony in the lower pasture. Smith'll show you where to bunk tonight, an' you kin hev your breakfast in the mornin'. S'long!" The ranch superintendent turned back to the paper in his hand which he had been discussing with his employer at the moment of the interruption. He had volleyed his instructions at Bridge as though pouring a rain of lead from a machine gun, and now that he had said what he had to say the incident was closed in so far as he was concerned.

The hospitality of the Southwest permitted no stranger to be turned away without food and a night's lodging. Grayson having arranged for these felt that he had done all that might be expected of a host, especially when the uninvited guest was so obviously a hobo and doubtless a horse thief as well, for who ever knew a hobo to own a horse?

Bridge continued to sit where he had reined in his pony. He was looking at Grayson with what the discerning boss judged to be politely concealed enjoyment.

"Possibly," suggested the boss in a whisper to his aide, "the man has business with you. You did not ask him, and I am sure that he said nothing about wishing a meal or a place to sleep."

"Huh?" grunted Grayson, and then to Bridge, "Well, what the devil *do* you want?"

"A job," replied Bridge, "or, to be more explicit, I need a job — far be it from me to *wish* one."

The Easterner smiled. Grayson looked a bit mystified — and irritated.

"Well, I hain't got none," he snapped. "We don't need nobody now unless it might be a good puncher — one who can rope and ride."

"I can ride," replied Bridge, "as is evidenced by the fact that you now see me astride a horse."

"I said *ride*," said Grayson. "Any fool can *sit* on a horse. *No*, I hain't got nothin', an' I'm busy now. Hold on!" he exclaimed as though seized by a sudden inspiration. He looked sharply at Bridge for a moment and then shook his head sadly. "No, I'm afraid you couldn't do it — a guy's got to be eddicated for the job I got in mind."

"Washing dishes?" suggested Bridge.

Grayson ignored the playfulness of the other's question.

"Keepin' books," he explained. There was a finality in his tone which said: "As you, of course, cannot keep books the interview is now over. Get out!"

"I could try," said Bridge. "I can read and write, you know. Let me try." Bridge wanted money for the trip to Rio, and, too, he wanted to stay in the country until Billy was ready to leave.

"Savvy Spanish?" asked Grayson.

"I read and write it better than I speak it," said Bridge, "though I do the latter well enough to get along anywhere that it is spoken."

Grayson wanted a bookkeeper worse than he could ever recall having wanted anything before in all his life. His better judgment told him that it was the height of idiocy to employ a ragged bum as a bookkeeper; but the bum was at least as much of a hope to him as is a straw to a drowning man, and so Grayson clutched at him.

"Go an' turn your cayuse in an' then come back here," he directed, "an' I'll give you a tryout."

"Thanks," said Bridge, and rode off in the direction of the pasture gate.

"'Fraid he won't never do," said Grayson, ruefully, after Bridge had passed out of earshot.

"I rather imagine that he will," said the boss. "He is an educated man, Grayson — you can tell that from his English, which is excellent. He's probably one of the great army of down-and-outers. The world is full of them — poor devils. Give him a chance, Grayson, and anyway he adds another American to our force, and each one counts."

"Yes, that's right; but I hope you won't need 'em before you an' Miss Barbara go," said Grayson.

"I hope not, Grayson; but one can never tell with

conditions here such as they are. Have you any hope that you will be able to obtain a safe conduct for us from General Villa?"

"Oh, Villa'll give us the paper all right," said Grayson; "but it won't do us no good unless we don't meet nobody but Villa's men on the way out. This here Pesita's the critter I'm leery of. He's got it in for all Americans, and especially for El Orobo Rancho. You know we beat off a raid of his about six months ago — killed half a dozen of his men, an' he won't never forgive that. Villa can't spare a big enough force to give us safe escort to the border and he can't assure the safety of the train service. It looks mighty bad, sir — I don't see what in hell you came for."

"Neither do I, Grayson," agreed the boss; "but I'm here and we've got to make the best of it. All this may blow over — it has before — and we'll laugh at our fears in a few weeks."

"This thing that's happenin' now won't never blow over 'til the stars and stripes blow over Chihuahua," said Grayson with finality.

A few moments later Bridge returned to the office, having unsaddled his pony and turned it into the pasture.

"What's your name?" asked Grayson, preparing to enter it in his time book.

"Bridge," replied the new bookkeeper.

"'Nitials," snapped Grayson.

Bridge hesitated. "Oh, put me down as L. Bridge," he said.

"Where from?" asked the ranch foreman.

"El Orobo Rancho," answered Bridge.

Grayson shot a quick glance at the man. The answer confirmed his suspicions that the stranger was probably a horse thief, which, in Grayson's estimation, was the worst thing a man could be.

"Where did you get that pony you come in on?" he demanded. "I ain't sayin' nothin' of course, but I jest want to tell you that we ain't got no use for horse thieves here."

The Easterner, who had been a listener, was shocked by the brutality of Grayson's speech; but Bridge only laughed.

"If you must know," he said, "I never bought that horse, an' the man he belonged to didn't give him to me. I just took him."

"You got your nerve," growled Grayson. "I guess you better git out. We don't want no horse thieves here."

"Wait," interposed the boss. "This man doesn't act like a horse thief. A horse thief, I should imagine, would scarcely admit his guilt. Let's have his story before we judge him."

"All right," said Grayson; "but he's just admitted he stole the horse."

Bridge turned to the boss. "Thanks," he said; "but really I did steal the horse."

Grayson made a gesture which said: "See, I told you so."

"It was like this," went on Bridge. "The gentleman who owned the horse, together with some of his friends, had been shooting at me and my friends. When it was all over there was no one left to inform us who were the legal heirs of the late owners of this and several other horses which were left upon our hands, so I borrowed this one. The law would say, doubtless, that I had stolen it; but I am perfectly willing to return it to its rightful owners if someone will find them for me."

"You been in a scrap?" asked Grayson. "Who with?"

"A party of Pesita's men," replied Bridge.

"When?"

"Yesterday."

"You see they are working pretty close," said Grayson, to his employer, and then to Bridge: "Well, if you took that cayuse from one of Pesita's bunch you can't call that stealin'. Your room's in there, back of the office, an' you'll find some clothes there that the last man forgot to take with him. You ken have 'em, an' from the looks o' yourn you need 'em."

"Thank you," replied Bridge. "My clothes are a bit rusty. I shall have to speak to James about them," and he passed through into the little bedroom off the office, and closed the door behind him.

"James?" grunted Grayson. "Who the devil does he mean by James? I hain't seen but one of 'em."

The boss was laughing quietly.

"The man's a character," he said. "He'll be worth all you pay him — if you can appreciate him, which I doubt, Grayson."

"I ken appreciate him if he ken keep books," replied Grayson. "That's all I ask of him."

When Bridge emerged from the bedroom he was clothed in white duck trousers, a soft shirt, and a pair of tennis shoes, and such a change had they wrought in his appearance that neither Grayson nor his employer would have known him had they not seen him come from the room into which they had sent him to make the exchange of clothing.

"Feel better?" asked the boss, smiling.

"Clothes are but an incident with me," replied Bridge. "I wear them because it is easier to do so than it would be to dodge the weather and the police. Whatever I may have upon my back affects in no way what I have within my head. No, I cannot say that I feel any better, since these clothes are not as comfortable as my old ones. However if it pleases Mr. Grayson that I should wear a pink kimono while working for him I shall gladly wear a pink kimono. What shall I do first, sir?" The question was directed toward Grayson.

"Sit down here an' see what you ken make of this bunch of trouble," replied the foreman. "I'll talk with you again this evenin'."

As Grayson and his employer quitted the office and walked together toward the corrals the latter's brow was corrugated by thought and his facial expression that of one who labors to fasten upon a baffling and illusive recollection.

"It beats all, Grayson," be said presently; "but I am sure that I have known this new bookkeeper of yours before. The moment he came out of that room dressed like a human being I knew that I had known him; but for the life of me I can't place him. I should be willing to wager considerable, however, that his name is not Bridge."

"S'pect you're right," assented Grayson. "He's probably one o' them eastern dude bank clerks what's gone wrong and come down here to hide. Mighty fine place to hide jest now, too.

"And say, speakin' of banks," he went on, "what'll I do 'bout sendin' over to Cuivaca fer the pay tomorrow. Next day's pay day. I don't like to send this here bum, I can't trust a greaser no better, an' I can't spare none of my white men thet I ken trust."

"Send him with a couple of the most trustworthy Mexicans you have," suggested the boss.

"There ain't no sich critter," replied Grayson; "but I guess that's the best I ken do. I'll send him along with Tony an' Benito — they hate each other too much to frame up anything together, an' they both hate a gringo. I reckon they'll hev a lovely trip."

"But they'll get back with the money, eh?" queried the boss.

"If Pesita don't get 'em," replied Grayson.

Chapter X

BILLY CRACKS A SAFE

*B*illy Byrne, captain, rode into Cuivaca from the south. He had made a wide detour in order to accomplish this; but under the circumstances he had thought it wise to do so. In his pocket was a safe conduct from one of Villa's generals farther south — a safe conduct taken by Pesita from the body of one of his recent victims. It would explain Billy's presence in Cuivaca since it had been intended to carry its rightful possessor to Juarez and across the border into the United States.

He found the military establishment at Cuivaca small and ill commanded. There were soldiers upon the streets; but the only regularly detailed guard was stationed in front of the bank. No one questioned Billy. He did not have to show his safe conduct.

"This looks easy," thought Billy. "A reg'lar skinch."

He first attended to his horse, turning him into a public corral, and then sauntered up the street to the bank, which he entered, still unquestioned. Inside he

changed a bill of large denomination which Pesita had
given him for the purpose of an excuse to examine the
lay of the bank from the inside. Billy took a long time
to count the change. All the time his eyes wandered
about the interior while he made mental notes of such
salient features as might prove of moment to him later.
The money counted Billy slowly rolled a cigarette.

He saw that the bank was roughly divided into two
sections by a wire and wood partition. On one side
were the customers, on the other the clerks and a teller.
The latter sat behind a small wicket through which he
received deposits and cashed checks. Back of him,
against the wall, stood a large safe of American manufacture. Billy had had business before with similar
safes. A doorway in the rear wall led into the yard
behind the building. It was closed by a heavy door
covered with sheet iron and fastened by several bolts
and a thick, strong bar. There were no windows in the
rear wall. From that side the bank appeared almost
impregnable to silent assault.

Inside everything was primitive and Billy found
himself wondering how a week passed without seeing
a bank robbery in the town. Possibly the strong rear
defenses and the armed guard in front accounted for
it.

Satisfied with what he had learned he passed out
onto the sidewalk and crossed the street to a saloon.
Some soldiers and citizens were drinking at little tables
in front of the bar. A couple of card games were in
progress, and through the open rear doorway Billy saw
a little gathering encircling a cock fight.

In none of these things was Billy interested. What
he had wished in entering the saloon was merely an
excuse to place himself upon the opposite side of the
street from the bank that he might inspect the front
from the outside without arousing suspicion.

Having purchased and drunk a bottle of poor beer, the temperature of which had probably never been below eighty since it left the bottling department of the Texas brewery which inflicted it upon the ignorant, he sauntered to the front window and looked out.

There he saw that the bank building was a two-story affair, the entrance to the second story being at the left side of the first floor, opening directly onto the sidewalk in full view of the sentry who paced to and fro before the structure.

Billy wondered what the second floor was utilized for. He saw soiled hangings at the windows which aroused a hope and a sudden inspiration. There was a sign above the entrance to the second floor; but Billy's knowledge of the language had not progressed sufficiently to permit him to translate it, although he had his suspicions as to its meaning. He would learn if his guess was correct.

Returning to the bar he ordered another bottle of beer, and as he drank it he practiced upon the bartender some of his recently acquired Spanish and learned, though not without considerable difficulty, that he might find lodgings for the night upon the second floor of the bank building.

Much elated, Billy left the saloon and walked along the street until he came to the one general store of the town. After another heart rending scrimmage with the language of Ferdinand and Isabella he succeeded in making several purchases — two heavy sacks, a brace, two bits, and a keyhole saw. Placing the tools in one of the sacks he wrapped the whole in the second sack and made his way back to the bank building.

Upon the second floor he found the proprietor of the rooming-house and engaged a room in the rear of the building, overlooking the yard. The layout was eminently satisfactory to Captain Byrne and it was

with a feeling of great self-satisfaction that he descended and sought a restaurant.

He had been sent by Pesita merely to look over the
ground and the defenses of the town, that the outlaw
might later ride in with his entire force and loot the
bank; but Billy Byrne, out of his past experience in
such matters, had evolved a much simpler plan for
separating the enemy from his wealth.

Having eaten, Billy returned to his room. It was now
dark and the bank closed and unlighted showed that
all had left it. Only the sentry paced up and down the
sidewalk in front.

Going at once to his room Billy withdrew his tools
from their hiding place beneath the mattress, and a
moment later was busily engaged in boring holes
through the floor at the foot of his bed. For an hour
he worked, cautiously and quietly, until he had a rough
circle of holes enclosing a space about two feet in
diameter. Then he laid aside the brace and bit, and
took the keyhole saw, with which he patiently sawed
through the wood between contiguous holes, until, the
circle completed, he lifted out a section of the floor
leaving an aperture large enough to permit him to
squeeze his body through when the time arrived for
him to pass into the bank beneath.

While Billy had worked three men had ridden into
Cuivaca. They were Tony, Benito, and the new bookkeeper of El Orobo Rancho. The Mexicans, after eat-
ing, repaired at once to the joys of the cantina; while
Bridge sought a room in the building to which his
escort directed him.

As chance would have it, it was the same building in
which Billy labored and the room lay upon the rear
side of it overlooking the same yard. But Bridge did
not lie awake to inspect his surroundings. For years he
had not ridden as many miles as he had during the

past two days, so that long unused muscles cried out for rest and relaxation. As a result, Bridge was asleep almost as soon as his head touched the pillow, and so profound was his slumber that it seemed that nothing short of a convulsion of nature would arouse him.

As Bridge lay down upon his bed Billy Byrne left his room and descended to the street. The sentry before the bank paid no attention to him, and Billy passed along, unhindered, to the corral where he had left his horse. Here, as he was saddling the animal, he was accosted, much to his disgust, by the proprietor.

in broken English the man expressed surprise that Billy rode out so late at night, and the American thought that he detected something more than curiosity in the other's manner and tone — suspicion of the strange gringo.

It would never do to leave the fellow in that state of mind, and so Billy leaned close to the other's ear, and with a broad grin and a wink whispered: "Senorita," and jerked his thumb toward the south. "I'll be back by mornin'," he added.

The Mexican's manner altered at once. He laughed and nodded, knowingly, and poked Billy in the ribs. Then he watched him mount and ride out of the corral toward the south — which was also in the direction of the bank, to the rear of which Billy rode without effort to conceal his movements.

There he dismounted and left his horse standing with the bridle reins dragging upon the ground, while he removed the lariat from the pommel of the saddle, and, stuffing it inside his shirt, walked back to the street on which the building stood, and so made his way past the sentry and to his room.

Here he pushed back the bed which he had drawn over the hole in the floor, dropped his two sacks through into the bank, and tying the brace to one end of the lariat lowered it through after the sacks.

Looping the middle of the lariat over a bedpost Billy grasped both strands firmly and lowered himself through the aperture into the room beneath. He made no more noise in his descent than he had made upon other similar occasions in his past life when he had practiced the gentle art of porch-climbing along Ashland Avenue and Washington Boulevard.

Having gained the floor he pulled upon one end of the lariat until he had drawn it free of the bedpost above, when it fell into his waiting hands. Coiling it carefully Billy placed it around his neck and under one arm. Billy, acting as a professional, was a careful and methodical man. He always saw that every little detail was properly attended to before he went on to the next phase of his endeavors. Because of this ingrained caution Billy had long since secured the tops of the two sacks together, leaving only a sufficient opening to permit of their each being filled without delay or inconvenience.

Now he turned his attention to the rear door. The bar and bolts were easily shot from their seats from the inside, and Billy saw to it that this was attended to before he went further with his labors. It were well to have one's retreat assured at the earliest possible moment. A single bolt Billy left in place that he might not be surprised by an intruder; but first he had tested it and discovered that it could be drawn with ease.

These matters satisfactorily attended to Billy assaulted the combination knob of the safe with the metal bit which he had inserted in the brace before lowering it into the bank.

The work was hard and progressed slowly. It was necessary to withdraw the bit often and lubricate it with a piece of soap which Billy had brought along in his pocket for the purpose; but eventually a hole was bored through into the tumblers of the combination lock.

From without Billy could hear the footsteps of the sentry pacing back and forth within fifty feet of him, all unconscious that the bank he was guarding was being looted almost beneath his eyes. Once a corporal came with another soldier and relieved the sentry. After that Billy heard the footfalls no longer, for the new sentry was barefoot.

The boring finished, Billy drew a bit of wire from an inside pocket and inserted it in the hole. Then, working the wire with accustomed fingers, he turned the combination knob this way and that, feeling with the bit of wire until the tumblers should all be in line.

This, too, was slow work; but it was infinitely less liable to attract attention than any other method of safe cracking with which Billy was familiar.

It was long past midnight when Captain Byrne was rewarded with success — the tumblers clicked into position, the handle of the safe door turned and the bolts slipped back.

To swing open the door and transfer the contents of the safe to the two sacks was the work of but a few minutes. As Billy rose and threw the heavy burden across a shoulder he heard a challenge from without, and then a parley. Immediately after the sound of footsteps ascending the stairway to the rooming-house came plainly to his ears, and then he had slipped the last bolt upon the rear door and was out in the yard beyond.

Now Bridge, sleeping the sleep of utter exhaustion that the boom of a cannon might not have disturbed, did that inexplicable thing which every one of us has done a hundred times in our lives. He awakened, with a start, out of a sound sleep, though no disturbing noise had reached his ears.

Something impelled him to sit up in bed, and as he did so he could see through the window beside him into the yard at the rear of the building. There in the moonlight he saw a man throwing a sack across the horn of a saddle. He saw the man mount, and he saw him wheel his horse around about and ride away toward the north. There seemed to Bridge nothing unusual about the man's act, nor had there been any indication either of stealth or haste to arouse the American's suspicions. Bridge lay back again upon his pillows and sought to woo the slumber which the sudden awakening seemed to have banished for the remainder of the night.

And up the stairway to the second floor staggered Tony and Benito. Their money was gone; but they had acquired something else which appeared much more difficult to carry and not so easily gotten rid of.

Tony held the key to their room. It was the second room upon the right of the hall. Tony remembered that very distinctly. He had impressed it upon his mind before leaving the room earlier in the evening, for Tony had feared some such contingency as that which had befallen.

Tony fumbled with the handle of a door, and stabbed vainly at an elusive keyhole.

"Wait," mumbled Benito. "This is not the room. It was the second door from the stairway. This is the third."

Tony lurched about and staggered back. Tony reasoned: "If that was the third door the next behind me must be the second, and on the right;" but Tony took not into consideration that he had reversed the direction of his erratic wobbling. He lunged across the hall — not because he wished to but because the spirits moved him. He came in contact with a door. "This, then, must be the second door," he soliloquized, "and it is upon my right. Ah, Benito, this is the room!"

Benito was skeptical. He said as much; but Tony was obdurate. Did he not know a second door when he saw one? Was he, furthermore, not a grown man and therefore entirely capable of distinguishing between his left hand and his right? Yes! Tony was all of that, and more, so Tony inserted the key in the lock — it would have turned any lock upon the second floor — and, lo! the door swung inward upon its hinges.

"Ah! Benito," cried Tony. "Did I not tell you so? See! This is our room, for the key opens the door."

The room was dark. Tony, carried forward by the weight of his head, which had long since grown unaccountably heavy, rushed his feet rapidly forward that he might keep them within a few inches of his center of equilibrium.

The distance which it took his feet to catch up with his head was equal to the distance between the doorway and the foot of the bed, and when Tony reached that spot, with Benito meandering after him, the latter, much to his astonishment, saw in the diffused moonlight which pervaded the room, the miraculous disappearance of his former enemy and erstwhile friend. Then from the depths below came a wild scream and a heavy thud.

The sentry upon the beat before the bank heard both. For an instant he stood motionless, then he called aloud for the guard, and turned toward the bank door. But this was locked and he could but peer in through the windows. Seeing a dark form within, and being a Mexican he raised his rifle and fired through the glass of the doors.

Tony, who had dropped through the hole which Billy had used so quietly, heard the zing of a bullet pass his head, and the impact as it sploshed into the adobe wall behind him. With a second yell Tony dodged behind the safe and besought Mary to protect him.

From above Benito peered through the hole into the blackness below. Down the hall came the barefoot landlord, awakened by the screams and the shot. Behind him came Bridge, buckling his revolver belt about his hips as he ran. Not having been furnished with pajamas Bridge had not thought it necessary to remove his clothing, and so he had lost no time in dressing.

When the two, now joined by Benito, reached the street they found the guard there, battering in the bank doors. Benito, fearing for the life of Tony, which if anyone took should be taken by him, rushed upon the sergeant of the guard, explaining with both lips and hands the remarkable accident which had precipitated Tony into the bank.

The sergeant listened, though he did not believe, and when the doors had fallen in, he commanded Tony to come out with his hands above his head. Then followed an investigation which disclosed the looting of the safe, and the great hole in the ceiling through which Tony had tumbled.

The bank president came while the sergeant and the landlord were in Billy's room investigating. Bridge had followed them.

"It was the gringo," cried the excited Boniface. "This is his room. He has cut a hole in my floor which I shall have to pay to have repaired."

A captain came next, sleepy-eyed and profane. When he heard what had happened and that the wealth which he had been detailed to guard had been taken while he slept, he tore his hair and promised that the sentry should be shot at dawn.

By the time they had returned to the street all the male population of Cuivaca was there and most of the female.

"One-thousand dollars," cried the bank president,

"to the man who stops the thief and returns to me what the villain has stolen."

A detachment of soldiers was in the saddle and passing the bank as the offer was made.

"Which way did he go?" asked the captain. "Did no one see him leave?"

Bridge was upon the point of saying that he had seen him and that he had ridden north, when it occurred to him that a thousand dollars — even a thousand dollars Mex — was a great deal of money, and that it would carry both himself and Billy to Rio and leave something for pleasure beside.

Then up spoke a tall, thin man with the skin of a coffee bean.

"I saw him, Senor Capitan," he cried. "He kept his horse in my corral, and at night he came and took it out saying that he was riding to visit a senorita. He fooled me, the scoundrel; but I will tell you — he rode south. I saw him ride south with my own eyes."

"Then we shall have him before morning," cried the captain, "for there is but one place to the south where a robber would ride, and he has not had sufficient start of us that he can reach safety before we overhaul him. Forward! March!" and the detachment moved down the narrow street. "Trot! March!" And as they passed the store: "Gallop! March!"

Bridge almost ran the length of the street to the corral. His pony must be rested by now, and a few miles to the north the gringo whose capture meant a thousand dollars to Bridge was on the road to liberty.

"I hate to do it," thought Bridge; "because, even if he is a bank robber, he's an American; but I need the money and in all probability the fellow is a scoundrel who should have been hanged long ago."

Over the trail to the north rode Captain Billy Byrne, secure in the belief that no pursuit would develop until after the opening hour of the bank in the morning, by which time he would be halfway on his return journey to Pesita's camp.

"Ol' man Pesita'll be some surprised when I show him what I got for him," mused Billy. "Say!" he exclaimed suddenly and aloud, "Why the devil should I take all this swag back to that yellow-faced yegg? Who pulled this thing off anyway? Why me, of course, and does anybody think Billy Byrne's boob enough to split with a guy that didn't have a hand in it at all. Split! Why the nut'll take it all!

"Nix! Me for the border. I couldn't do a thing with all this coin down in Rio, an' Bridgie'll be along there most any time. We can hit it up some in lil' ol' Rio on this bunch o' dough. Why, say kid, there must be a million here, from the weight of it."

A frown suddenly clouded his face. "Why did I take it?" he asked himself. "Was I crackin' a safe, or was I pullin' off something fine fer poor, bleedin' Mexico? If I was a-doin' that they ain't nothin' criminal in what I done — except to the guy that owned the coin. If I was just plain crackin' a safe on my own hook why then I'm a crook again an' I can't be that — no, not with that face of yours standin' out there so plain right in front of me, just as though you were there yourself, askin' me to remember an' be decent. God! Barbara — why wasn't I born for the likes of you, and not just a measly, ornery mucker like I am. Oh, hell! what is that that Bridge sings of Knibbs's:

> There ain't no sweet Penelope somewhere that's
>   longing much for me,
> But I can smell the blundering sea, and hear the rig-
>   ging hum;
> And I can hear the whispering lips that fly before
>   the out-bound ships,

And I can hear the breakers on the sand a-calling
  "Come!"

Billy took off his hat and scratched his head.

"Funny," he thought, "how a girl and poetry can get
a tough nut like me. I wonder what the guys that used
to hang out in back of Kelly's 'ud say if they seen what
was goin' on in my bean just now. They'd call me Lizzy,
eh? Well, they wouldn't call me Lizzy more'n once. I
may be gettin' soft in the head, but I'm all to the good
with my dukes."

Speed is not conducive to sentimental thoughts and
so Billy had unconsciously permitted his pony to drop
into a lazy walk. There was no need for haste anyhow.
No one knew yet that the bank had been robbed, or at
least so Billy argued. He might, however, have thought
differently upon the subject of haste could he have had
a glimpse of the horseman in his rear — two miles
behind him, now, but rapidly closing up the distance
at a keen gallop, while he strained his eyes across the
moonlit flat ahead in eager search for his quarry.

So absorbed was Billy Byrne in his reflections that
his ears were deaf to the pounding of the hoofs of the
pursuer's horse upon the soft dust of the dry road until
Bridge was little more than a hundred yards from him.
For the last half-mile Bridge had had the figure of the
fugitive in full view and his mind had been playing
rapidly with seductive visions of the one-thousand
dollars reward — one-thousand dollars Mex, perhaps,
but still quite enough to excite pleasant thoughts. At
the first glimpse of the horseman ahead Bridge had
reined his mount down to a trot that the noise of his
approach might thereby be lessened. He had drawn his
revolver from its holster, and was upon the point of
putting spurs to his horse for a sudden dash upon the
fugitive when the man ahead, finally attracted by the

noise of the other's approach, turned in his saddle and saw him.

Neither recognized the other, and at Bridge's command of, "Hands up!" Billy, lightning-like in his quickness, drew and fired. The bullet raked Bridge's hat from his head but left him unscathed.

Billy had wheeled his pony around until he stood broadside toward Bridge. The latter fired scarce a second after Billy's shot had pinged so perilously close — fired at a perfect target but fifty yards away.

At the sound of the report the robber's horse reared and plunged, then, wheeling and tottering high upon its hind feet, fell backward. Billy, realizing that his mount had been hit, tried to throw himself from the saddle; but until the very moment that the beast toppled over the man was held by his cartridge belt which, as the animal first lunged, had caught over the high horn of the Mexican saddle.

The belt slipped from the horn as the horse was falling, and Billy succeeded in throwing himself a little to one side. One leg, however, was pinned beneath the animal's body and the force of the fall jarred the revolver from Billy's hand to drop just beyond his reach.

His carbine was in its boot at the horse's side, and the animal was lying upon it. Instantly Bridge rode to his side and covered him with his revolver.

"Don't move," he commanded, "or I'll be under the painful necessity of terminating your earthly endeavors right here and now."

"Well, for the love o' Mike!" cried the fallen bandit "You?"

Bridge was off his horse the instant that the familiar voice sounded in his ears.

"Billy!" he exclaimed. "Why — Billy — was it you who robbed the bank?"

Even as he spoke Bridge was busy easing the weight of the dead pony from Billy's leg.

"Anything broken?" he asked as the bandit struggled to free himself.

"Not so you could notice it," replied Billy, and a moment later he was on his feet. "Say, bo," he added, "it's a mighty good thing you dropped little pinto here, for I'd a sure got you my next shot. Gee! it makes me sweat to think of it. But about this bank robbin' business. You can't exactly say that I robbed a bank. That money was the enemy's resources, an' I just nicked their resources. That's war. That ain't robbery. I ain't takin' it for myself — it's for the cause — the cause o' poor, bleedin' Mexico," and Billy grinned a large grin.

"You took it for Pesita?" asked Bridge.

"Of course," replied Billy. "I won't get a jitney of it. I wouldn't take none of it, Bridge, honest. I'm on the square now."

"I know you are, Billy," replied the other; "but if you're caught you might find it difficult to convince the authorities of your highmindedness and your disinterestedness."

"Authorities!" scoffed Billy. "There ain't no authorities in Mexico. One bandit is just as good as another, and from Pesita to Carranza they're all bandits at heart. They ain't a one of 'em that gives two whoops in hell for poor, bleedin' Mexico — unless they can do the bleedin' themselves. It's dog eat dog here. If they caught me they'd shoot me whether I'd robbed their bank or not. What's that?" Billy was suddenly alert, straining his eyes back in the direction of Cuivaca.

"They're coming, Billy," said Bridge. "Take my horse — quick! You must get out of here in a hurry. The whole post is searching for you. I thought that they went toward the south, though. Some of them must have circled."

"What'll you do if I take your horse?" asked Billy.

"I can walk back," said Bridge, "it isn't far to town. I'll tell them that I had come only a short distance when my horse threw me and ran away. They'll believe it for they think I'm a rotten horseman — the two vaqueros who escorted me to town I mean."

Billy hesitated. "I hate to do it, Bridge," he said.

"You must, Billy," urged the other.

"If they find us here together it'll merely mean that the two of us will get it, for I'll stick with you, Billy, and we can't fight off a whole troop of cavalry out here in the open. If you take my horse we can both get out of it, and later I'll see you in Rio. Good-bye, Billy, I'm off for town," and Bridge turned and started back along the road on foot.

Billy watched him in silence for a moment. The truth of Bridge's statement of fact was so apparent that Billy was forced to accept the plan. A moment later he transferred the bags of loot to Bridge's pony, swung into the saddle, and took a last backward look at the diminishing figure of the man swinging along in the direction of Cuivaca.

"Say," he muttered to himself; "but you're a right one, bo," and wheeling to the north he clapped his spurs to his new mount and loped easily off into the night.

Chapter XI

BARBARA RELEASES A CONSPIRATOR

*I*t was a week later, yet Grayson still was growling about the loss of "that there Brazos pony." Grayson, the boss, and the boss's daughter were sitting upon the veranda of the ranchhouse when the foreman reverted to the subject.

"I knew I didn't have no business hirin' a man thet can't ride," he said. "Why thet there Brazos pony never did stumble, an' if he'd of stumbled he'd a-stood aroun' a year waitin' to be caught up agin. I jest cain't figger it out no ways how thet there tenderfoot bookkeeper lost him. He must a-shooed him away with a stick. An' saddle an' bridle an' all gone too. Doggone it!"

"I'm the one who should be peeved," spoke up the girl with a wry smile. "Brazos was my pony. He's the one you picked out for me to ride while I am here; but I am sure poor Mr. Bridge feels as badly about it as anyone, and I know that he couldn't help it. We shouldn't be too hard on him. We might just as well attempt to hold him responsible for the looting of the bank and the loss of the pay-roll money."

"Well," said Grayson, "I give him thet horse 'cause I knew he couldn't ride, an' thet was the safest horse in the cavvy. I wisht I'd given him Santa Anna instid — I wouldn't a-minded losin' him. There won't no one ride him anyhow he's thet ornery."

"The thing that surprises me most," remarked the boss, "is that Brazos doesn't come back. He was foaled on this range, and he's never been ridden anywhere else, has he?"

"He was foaled right here on this ranch," Grayson corrected him, "and he ain't never been more'n a hundred mile from it. If he ain't dead or stolen he'd a-ben back afore the bookkeeper was. It's almighty queer."

"What sort of bookkeeper is Mr. Bridge?" asked the girl.

"Oh, he's all right I guess," replied Grayson grudgingly. "A feller's got to be some good at something. He's probably one of these here paper-collar, cracker-fed college dudes thet don't know nothin' else 'cept writin' in books."

The girl rose, smiled, and moved away.

"I like Mr. Bridge, anyhow," she called back over her shoulder, "for whatever he may not be he is certainly a well-bred gentleman," which speech did not tend to raise Mr. Bridge in the estimation of the hard-fisted ranch foreman.

"Funny them greasers don't come in from the north range with thet bunch o' steers. They ben gone all day now," he said to the boss, ignoring the girl's parting sally.

Bridge sat tip-tilted against the front of the office

building reading an ancient magazine which he had
found within. His day's work was done and he was but
waiting for the gong that would call him to the evening
meal with the other employees of the ranch. The magazine failed to rouse his interest. He let it drop idly to
his knees and with eyes closed reverted to his never-
failing source of entertainment.

And then that slim, poetic guy he turned and
       looked me in the eye,
". . . It's overland and overland and overseas to —
       where?"
"Most anywhere that isn't here," I says. His face
       went kind of queer.
"The place we're in is always here. The other place is
       there."

Bridge stretched luxuriously. "'There,'" he repeated.
"I've been searching for *there* for many years; but for
some reason I can never get away from *here*. About two
weeks of any place on earth and that place is just plain
here to me, and I'm longing once again for *there*."

His musings were interrupted by a sweet feminine
voice close by. Bridge did not open his eyes at once —
he just sat there, listening.

As I was hiking past the woods, the cool and sleepy
       summer woods,
  I saw a guy a-talking to the sunshine in the air,
Thinks I, "He's going to have a fit — I'll stick
       around and watch a bit,"
  But he paid no attention, hardly knowing I was
       there.

Then the girl broke into a merry laugh and Bridge
opened his eyes and came to his feet.

"I didn't know you cared for that sort of stuff," he said. "Knibbs writes man-verse. I shouldn't have imagined that it would appeal to a young lady."

"But it does, though," she replied; "at least to me. There's a swing to it and a freedom that 'gets me in the eye.'"

Again she laughed, and when this girl laughed, harder-headed and much older men than Mr. L. Bridge felt strange emotions move within their breasts.

For a week Barbara had seen a great deal of the new bookkeeper. Aside from her father he was the only man of culture and refinement of which the rancho could boast, or, as the rancho would have put it, be ashamed of.

She had often sought the veranda of the little office and lured the new bookkeeper from his work, and on several occasions had had him at the ranchhouse. Not only was he an interesting talker; but there was an element of mystery about him which appealed to the girl's sense of romance.

She knew that he was a gentleman born and reared, and she often found herself wondering what tragic train of circumstances had set him adrift among the flotsam of humanity's wreckage. Too, the same persistent conviction that she had known him somewhere in the past that possessed her father clung to her mind; but she could not place him.

"I overheard your dissertation on *here and there,*" said the girl. "I could not very well help it — it would have been rude to interrupt a conversation." Her eyes sparkled mischievously and her cheeks dimpled.

"You wouldn't have been interrupting a conversation," objected Bridge, smiling; "you would have been turning a monologue into a conversation."

"But it was a conversation," insisted the girl. "The wanderer was conversing with the bookkeeper. You are a victim of wanderlust, Mr. L. Bridge — don't deny it. You hate bookkeeping, or any other such prosaic vocation as requires permanent residence in one place."

"Come now," expostulated the man. "That is hardly fair. Haven't I been here a whole week?"

They both laughed.

"What in the world can have induced you to remain so long?" cried Barbara. "How very much like an old timer you must feel — one of the oldest inhabitants."

"I am a regular aborigine," declared Bridge; but his heart would have chosen another reply. It would have been glad to tell the girl that there was a very real and a very growing inducement to remain at El Orobo Rancho. The man was too self-controlled, however, to give way to the impulses of his heart.

At first he had just liked the girl, and been immensely glad of her companionship because there was so much that was common to them both — a love for good music, good pictures, and good literature — things Bridge hadn't had an opportunity to discuss with another for a long, long time.

And slowly he had found delight in just sitting and looking at her. He was experienced enough to realize that this was a dangerous symptom, and so from the moment he had been forced to acknowledge it to himself he had been very careful to guard his speech and his manner in the girl's presence.

He found pleasure in dreaming of what might have been as he sat watching the girl's changing expression as different moods possessed her; but as for permitting a hope, even, of realization of his dreams — ah, he was far too practical for that, dreamer though he was.

As the two talked Grayson passed. His rather stern face clouded as he saw the girl and the new bookkeeper laughing there together.

"Ain't you got nothin' to do?" he asked Bridge.

"Yes, indeed," replied the latter.

"Then why don't you do it?" snapped Grayson.

"I am," said Bridge.

"Mr. Bridge is entertaining me," interrupted the girl, before Grayson could make any rejoinder. "It is my fault — I took him from his work. You don't mind, do you, Mr. Grayson?"

Grayson mumbled an inarticulate reply and went his way.

"Mr. Grayson does not seem particularly enthusiastic about me," laughed Bridge.

"No," replied the girl, candidly; "but I think it's just because you can't ride."

"Can't ride!" ejaculated Bridge. "Why, haven't I been riding ever since I came here?"

"Mr. Grayson doesn't consider anything in the way of equestrianism riding unless the ridden is perpetually seeking the life of the rider," explained Barbara. "Just at present he is terribly put out because you lost Brazos. He says Brazos never stumbled in his life, and even if you had fallen from his back he would have stood beside you waiting for you to remount him. You see he was the kindest horse on the ranch — especially picked for me to ride. However in the world *did* you lose him, Mr. Bridge?"

The girl was looking full at the man as she propounded her query. Bridge was silent. A faint flush overspread his face. He had not before known that the horse was hers. He couldn't very well tell her the truth, and he wouldn't lie to her, so he made no reply.

Barbara saw the flush and noted the man's silence. For the first time her suspicions were aroused, yet she would not believe that this gentle, amiable drifter could be guilty of any crime greater than negligence or carelessness. But why his evident embarrassment now? The girl was mystified. For a moment or two they sat in silence, then Barbara rose.

"I must run along back now," she explained. "Papa will be wondering what has become of me."

"Yes," said Bridge, and let her go. He would have been glad to tell her the truth; but he couldn't do that without betraying Billy. He had heard enough to know that Francisco Villa had been so angered over the bold looting of the bank in the face of a company of his own soldiers that he would stop at nothing to secure the person of the thief once his identity was known. Bridge was perfectly satisfied with the ethics of his own act on the night of the bank robbery. He knew that the girl would have applauded him, and that Grayson himself would have done what Bridge did had a like emergency confronted the ranch foreman; but to have admitted complicity in the escape of the fugitive would have been to have exposed himself to the wrath of Villa, and at the same time revealed the identity of the thief. "Nor," thought Bridge, "would it get Brazos back for Barbara."

It was after dark when the vaqueros Grayson had sent to the north range returned to the ranch. They came empty-handed and slowly for one of them supported a wounded comrade on the saddle before him. They rode directly to the office where Grayson and Bridge were going over some of the business of the day, and when the former saw them his brow clouded for he knew before he heard their story what had happened.

"Who done it?" he asked, as the men filed into the office, half carrying the wounded man.

"Some of Pesita's followers," replied Benito.

"Did they git the steers, too?" inquired Grayson.

"Part of them — we drove off most and scattered them. We saw the Brazos pony, too," and Benito looked from beneath heavy lashes in the direction of the bookkeeper.

"Where?" asked Grayson.

"One of Pesita's officers rode him — an Americano. Tony and I saw this same man in Cuivaca the night the bank was robbed, and today he was riding the Brazos pony." Again the dark eyes turned toward Bridge.

Grayson was quick to catch the significance of the Mexican's meaning. The more so as it was directly in line with suspicions which he himself had been nursing since the robbery.

During the colloquy the boss entered the office. He had heard the returning vaqueros ride into the ranch and noting that they brought no steers with them had come to the office to hear their story. Barbara, spurred by curiosity, accompanied her father.

"You heard what Benito says?" asked Grayson, turning toward his employer

The latter nodded. All eyes were upon Bridge.

"Well," snapped Grayson, "what you gotta say fer yourself? I ben suspectin' you right along. I knew derned well that that there Brazos pony never run off by hisself. You an' that other crook from the States framed this whole thing up pretty slick, didn'tcha? Well, we'll —"

"Wait a moment, wait a moment, Grayson," interrupted the boss. "Give Mr. Bridge a chance to explain. You're making a rather serious charge against him without any particularly strong proof to back your accusation."

"Oh, that's all right," exclaimed Bridge, with a smile. "I have known that Mr. Grayson suspected me of implication in the robbery; but who can blame him — a man who can't ride might be guilty of almost anything."

Grayson sniffed. Barbara took a step nearer Bridge.

She had been ready to doubt him herself only an hour or so ago; but that was before he had been accused. Now that she found others arrayed against him her impulse was to come to his defense.

"You didn't do it, did you, Mr. Bridge?" Her tone was almost pleading.

"If you mean robbing the bank," he replied; "I did not Miss Barbara. I knew no more about it until after it was over than Benito or Tony — in fact they were the ones who discovered it while I was still asleep in my room above the bank."

"Well, how did the robber git thet there Brazos pony then?" demanded Grayson savagely. "Thet's what I want to know."

"You'll have to ask him, Mr. Grayson," replied Bridge.

"Villa'll ask him, when he gits holt of him," snapped Grayson; "but I reckon he'll git all the information out of you thet he wants first. He'll be in Cuivaca tomorrer, an' so will you."

"You mean that you are going to turn me over to General Villa?" asked Bridge. "You are going to turn an American over to that butcher knowing that he'll be shot inside of twenty-four hours?

"Shootin's too damned good fer a horse thief," replied Grayson.

Barbara turned impulsively toward her father. "You won't let Mr. Grayson do that?" she asked.

"Mr. Grayson knows best how to handle such an affair as this, Barbara," replied her father. "He is my superintendent, and I have made it a point never to interfere with him."

"You will let Mr. Bridge be shot without making an effort to save him?" she demanded.

"We do not know that he will be shot," replied the ranch owner. "If he is innocent there is no reason why

he should be punished. If he is guilty of implication
in the Cuivaca bank robbery he deserves, according to
the rules of war, to die, for General Villa, I am told,
considers that a treasonable act. Some of the funds
upon which his government depends for munitions of
war were there — they were stolen and turned over to
the enemies of Mexico."

"And if we interfere we'll turn Villa against us,"
interposed Grayson. "He ain't any too keen for Americans as it is. Why, if this fellow was my brother I'd hev
to turn him over to the authorities."

"Well, I thank God," exclaimed Bridge fervently,
"that in addition to being shot by Villa I don't have
to endure the added disgrace of being related to you,
and I'm not so sure that I shall be hanged by Villa,"
and with that he wiped the oil lamp from the table
against which he had been leaning, and leaped across
the room for the doorway.

Barbara and her father had been standing nearest the
exit, and as the girl realized the bold break for liberty
the man was making, she pushed her father to one side
and threw open the door.

Bridge was through it in an instant, with a parting,
"God bless you, little girl!" as he passed her. Then the
door was closed with a bang. Barbara turned the key,
withdrew it from the lock and threw it across the
darkened room.

Grayson and the unwounded Mexicans leaped after
the fugitive only to find their way barred by the locked
door. Outside Bridge ran to the horses standing patiently with lowered heads awaiting the return of their
masters. In an instant he was astride one of them, and
lashing the others ahead of him with a quirt he spurred
away into the night.

By the time Grayson and the Mexicans had wormed
their way through one of the small windows of the

office the new bookkeeper was beyond sight and ear-shot.

As the ranch foreman was saddling up with several of his men in the corral to give chase to the fugitive the boss strolled in and touched him on the arm.

"Mr. Grayson," he said, "I have made it a point never to interfere with you; but I am going to ask you now not to pursue Mr. Bridge. I shall be glad if he makes good his escape. Barbara was right — he is a fellow-American. We cannot turn him over to Villa, or any other Mexican to be murdered."

Grumblingly Grayson unsaddled. "Ef you'd seen what I've seen around here," he said, "I guess you wouldn't be so keen to save this feller's hide."

"What do you mean?" asked the boss.

"I mean that he's ben tryin' to make love to your daughter."

The older man laughed. "Don't be a fool, Grayson," he said, and walked away.

An hour later Barbara was strolling up and down before the ranchhouse in the cool and refreshing air of the Chihuahua night. Her mind was occupied with disquieting reflections of the past few hours. Her pride was immeasurably hurt by the part impulse had forced her to take in the affair at the office. Not that she regretted that she had connived in the escape of Bridge; but it was humiliating that a girl of her position should have been compelled to play so melodramatic a part before Grayson and his Mexican vaqueros.

Then, too, was she disappointed in Bridge. She had looked upon him as a gentleman whom misfortune and wanderlust had reduced to the lowest stratum of society. Now she feared that he belonged to that sub-stratum which lies below the lowest which society recognizes as a part of itself, and which is composed solely of the criminal class.

It was hard for Barbara to realize that she had associated with a thief — just for a moment it was hard, until recollection forced upon her the unwelcome fact of the status of another whom she had known — to whom she had given her love. The girl did not wince at the thought — instead she squared her shoulders and raised her chin.

"I am proud of him, whatever he may have been," she murmured; but she was not thinking of the new bookkeeper. When she did think again of Bridge it was to be glad that he had escaped — "for he is an American, like myself."

"Well!" exclaimed a voice behind her. "You played us a pretty trick, Miss Barbara."

The girl turned to see Grayson approaching. To her surprise he seemed to hold no resentment whatsoever. She greeted him courteously.

"I couldn't let you turn an American over to General Villa," she said, "no matter what he had done."

"I liked your spirit," said the man. "You're the kind o' girl I ben lookin' fer all my life — one with nerve an' grit, an' you got 'em both. You liked thet bookkeepin' critter, an' he wasn't half a man. I like you an' I am a man, ef I do say so myself."

The girl drew back in astonishment.

"Mr. Grayson!" she exclaimed. "You are forgetting yourself."

"No I ain't," he cried hoarsely. "I love you an' I'm goin' to have you. You'd love me too ef you knew me better."

He took a step forward and grasped her arm, trying to draw her to him. The girl pushed him away with one hand, and with the other struck him across the face.

Grayson dropped her arm, and as he did so she drew herself to her full height and looked him straight in the eyes.

"You may go now," she said, her voice like ice. "I shall never speak of this to anyone — provided you never attempt to repeat it."

The man made no reply. The blow in the face had cooled his ardor temporarily, but had it not also served another purpose? — to crystallize it into a firm and inexorable resolve.

When he had departed Barbara turned and entered the house.

Chapter XII

BILLY TO THE RESCUE

*I*t was nearly ten o'clock the following morning when Barbara, sitting upon the veranda of the ranchhouse, saw her father approaching from the direction of the office. His face wore a troubled expression which the girl could not but note.

"What's the matter, Papa?" she asked, as he sank into a chair at her side.

"Your self-sacrifice of last evening was all to no avail," he replied. "Bridge has been captured by Villistas."

"What?" cried the girl. "You can't mean it — how did you learn?"

"Grayson just had a phone message from Cuivaca," he explained. "They only repaired the line yesterday since Pesita's men cut it last month. This was our first message. And do you know, Barbara, I can't help feeling sorry. I had hoped that he would get away."

"So had I," said the girl.

Her father was eyeing her closely to note the effect

of his announcement upon her; but he could see no greater concern reflected than that which he himself felt for a fellow-man and an American who was doomed to death at the hands of an alien race, far from his own land and his own people.

"Can nothing be done?" she asked.

"Absolutely," he replied with finality. "I have talked it over with Grayson and he assures me that an attempt at intervention upon our part might tend to antagonize Villa, in which case we are all as good as lost. He is none too fond of us as it is, and Grayson believes, and not without reason, that he would welcome the slightest pretext for withdrawing the protection of his favor. Instantly he did that we should become the prey of every marauding band that infests the mountains. Not only would Pesita swoop down upon us, but those companies of freebooters which acknowledge nominal loyalty to Villa would be about our ears in no time. No, dear, we may do nothing. The young man has made his bed, and now I am afraid that he will have to lie in it alone."

For awhile the girl sat in silence, and presently her father arose and entered the house. Shortly after she followed him, reappearing soon in riding togs and walking rapidly to the corrals. Here she found an American cowboy busily engaged in whittling a stick as he sat upon an upturned cracker box and shot accurate streams of tobacco juice at a couple of industrious tumble bugs that had had the great impudence to roll their little ball of provender within the whittler's range.

"O Eddie!" she cried.

The man looked up, and was at once electrified into action. He sprang to his feet and whipped off his sombrero. A broad smile illumined his freckled face.

"Yes, miss," he answered. "What can I do for you?"

"Saddle a pony for me, Eddie," she explained. "I want to take a little ride."

"Sure!" he assured her cheerily. "Have it ready in a jiffy," and away he went, uncoiling his riata, toward the little group of saddle ponies which stood in the corral against necessity for instant use.

In a couple of minutes he came back leading one, which he tied to the corral bars.

"But I can't ride that horse," exclaimed the girl. "He bucks."

"Sure," said Eddie. "I'm a-goin' to ride him."

"Oh, are you going somewhere?" she asked.

"I'm goin' with you, miss," announced Eddie, sheepishly.

"But I didn't ask you, Eddie, and I don't want you — today," she urged.

"Sorry, miss," he threw back over his shoulder as he walked back to rope a second pony; "but them's orders. You're not to be allowed to ride no place without a escort. 'Twouldn't be safe neither, miss," he almost pleaded, "an' I won't hinder you none. I'll ride behind far enough to be there ef I'm needed."

Directly he came back with another pony, a sad-eyed, gentle-appearing little beast, and commenced saddling and bridling the two.

"Will you promise," she asked, after watching him in silence for a time, "that you will tell no one where I go or whom I see?"

"Cross my heart hope to die," he assured her.

"All right, Eddie, then I'll let you come with me, and you can ride beside me, instead of behind."

Across the flat they rode, following the windings of the river road, one mile, two, five, ten. Eddie had long since been wondering what the purpose of so steady a pace could be. This was no pleasure ride which took the boss's daughter — "heifer," Eddie would have called

her — ten miles up river at a hard trot. Eddie was
worried, too. They had passed the danger line, and were
well within the stamping ground of Pesita and his
retainers. Here each little adobe dwelling, and they were
scattered at intervals of a mile or more along the river,
contained a rabid partisan of Pesita, or it contained no
one — Pesita had seen to this latter condition personally.

At last the young lady drew rein before a squalid and
dilapidated hut. Eddie gasped. It was Jose's, and Jose
was a notorious scoundrel whom old age alone kept
from the active pursuit of the only calling he ever had
known — brigandage. Why should the boss's daughter
come to Jose? Jose was hand in glove with every cut-
throat in Chihuahua, or at least within a radius of two
hundred miles of his abode.

Barbara swung herself from the saddle, and handed
her bridle reins to Eddie.

"Hold him, please," she said. "I'll be gone but a
moment."

"You're not goin' in there to see old Jose alone?"
gasped Eddie.

"Why not?" she asked. "If you're afraid you can leave
my horse and ride along home."

Eddie colored to the roots of his sandy hair, and kept
silent. The girl approached the doorway of the mean
hovel and peered within. At one end sat a bent old
man, smoking. He looked up as Barbara's figure darkened the doorway.

"Jose!" said the girl.

The old man rose to his feet and came toward her.

"Eh? Senorita, eh?" he cackled.

"You are Jose?" she asked.

"Si, senorita," replied the old Indian. "What can
poor old Jose do to serve the beautiful senorita?"

"You can carry a message to one of Pesita's officers,"

replied the girl. "I have heard much about you since I came to Mexico. I know that there is not another man in this part of Chihuahua who may so easily reach Pesita as you." She raised her hand for silence as the Indian would have protested. Then she reached into the pocket of her riding breeches and withdrew a handful of silver which she permitted to trickle, tinklingly, from one palm to the other. "I wish you to go to the camp of Pesita," she continued, "and carry word to the man who robbed the bank at Cuivaca — he is an American — that his friend, Senor Bridge has been captured by Villa and is being held for execution in Cuivaca. You must go at once — you must get word to Senor Bridge's friend so that help may reach Senor Bridge before dawn. Do you understand?"

The Indian nodded assent.

"Here," said the girl, "is a payment on account. When I know that you delivered the message in time you shall have as much more. Will you do it?"

"I will try," said the Indian, and stretched forth a clawlike hand for the money.

"Good!" exclaimed Barbara. "Now start at once," and she dropped the silver coins into the old man's palm.

*I*t was dusk when Captain Billy Byrne was summoned to the tent of Pesita. There he found a weazened, old Indian squatting at the side of the outlaw.

"Jose," said Pesita, "has word for you."

Billy Byrne turned questioningly toward the Indian.

"I have been sent, Senor Capitan," explained Jose, "by the beautiful senorita of El Orobo Rancho to tell you that your friend, Senor Bridge, has been captured by General Villa, and is being held at Cuivaca, where he will doubtless be shot — if help does not reach him before tomorrow morning."

Pesita was looking questioningly at Byrne. Since the gringo had returned from Cuivaca with the loot of the bank and turned the last penny of it over to him the outlaw had looked upon his new captain as something just short of superhuman. To have robbed the bank thus easily while Villa's soldiers paced back and forth before the doorway seemed little short of an indication of miraculous powers, while to have turned the loot over intact to his chief, not asking for so much as a peso of it, was absolutely incredible.

Pesita could not understand this man; but he admired him greatly and feared him, too. Such a man was worth a hundred of the ordinary run of humanity that enlisted beneath Pesita's banners. Byrne had but to ask a favor to have it granted, and now, when he called upon Pesita to furnish him with a suitable force for the rescue of Bridge the brigand enthusiastically acceded to his demands.

"I will come," he exclaimed, "and all my men shall ride with me. We will take Cuivaca by storm. We may even capture Villa himself."

"Wait a minute, bo," interrupted Billy Byrne. "Don't get excited. I'm lookin' to get my pal outen' Cuivaca. After that I don't care who you capture; but I'm goin' to get Bridgie out first. I ken do it with twenty-five men — if it ain't too late. Then, if you want to, you can shoot up the town. Lemme have the twenty-five, an' you hang around the edges with the rest of 'em 'til I'm done. Whaddaya say?"

Pesita was willing to agree to anything, and so it came that half an hour later Billy Byrne was leading a choice selection of some two dozen cutthroats down through the hills toward Cuivaca. While a couple of miles in the rear followed Pesita with the balance of his band.

Billy rode until the few remaining lights of Cuivaca shone but a short distance ahead and they could hear plainly the strains of a grating graphophone from beyond the open windows of a dance hall, and the voices of the sentries as they called the hour.

"Stay here," said Billy to a sergeant at his side, "until you hear a hoot owl cry three times from the direction of the barracks and guardhouse, then charge the opposite end of the town, firing off your carbines like hell an' yellin' yer heads off. Make all the racket you can, an' keep it up 'til you get 'em comin' in your direction, see? Then turn an' drop back slowly, eggin' 'em on, but holdin' 'em to it as long as you can. Do you get me, bo?"

From the mixture of Spanish and English and Granavenooish the sergeant gleaned enough of the intent of his commander to permit him to salute and admit that he understood what was required of him.

Having given his instructions Billy Byrne rode off to the west, circled Cuivaca and came close up upon the southern edge of the little village. Here he dismounted and left his horse hidden behind an outbuilding, while he crept cautiously forward to reconnoiter.

He knew that the force within the village had no reason to fear attack. Villa knew where the main bodies of his enemies lay, and that no force could approach Cuivaca without word of its coming reaching the garrison many hours in advance of the foe. That Pesita, or another of the several bandit chiefs in the neighborhood would dare descend upon a garrisoned town never for a moment entered the calculations of the rebel leader.

For these reasons Billy argued that Cuivaca would be poorly guarded. On the night he had spent there he had seen sentries before the bank, the guardhouse, and the barracks in addition to one who paced to and fro in front of the house in which the commander of the garrison maintained his headquarters. Aside from these the town was unguarded.

Nor were conditions different tonight. Billy came within a hundred yards of the guardhouse before he discovered a sentinel. The fellow lolled upon his gun in front of the building — an adobe structure in the rear of the barracks. The other three sides of the guard-house appeared to be unwatched.

Billy threw himself upon his stomach and crawled slowly forward stopping often. The sentry seemed asleep. He did not move. Billy reached the shadow at the side of the structure and some fifty feet from the soldier without detection. Then he rose to his feet directly beneath a barred window.

Within Bridge paced back and forth the length of the little building. He could not sleep. Tomorrow he was to be shot! Bridge did not wish to die. That very morning General Villa in person had examined him. The general had been exceedingly wroth — the sting of the theft of his funds still irritated him; but he had given Bridge no inkling as to his fate. It had remained for a fellow-prisoner to do that. This man, a deserter, was to be shot, so he said, with Bridge, a fact which gave him an additional twenty-four hours of life, since, he asserted, General Villa wished to be elsewhere than in Cuivaca when an American was executed. Thus he could disclaim responsibility for the act.

The general was to depart in the morning. Shortly after, Bridge and the deserter would be led out and blindfolded before a stone wall — if there was such a thing, or a brick wall, or an adobe wall. It made little difference to the deserter, or to Bridge either. The wall was but a trivial factor. It might go far to add romance to whomever should read of the affair later; but in so far as Bridge and the deserter were concerned it meant nothing. A billboard, thought Bridge, bearing the slogan: "Eventually! Why not now?" would have been equally as efficacious and far more appropriate.

The room in which he was confined was stuffy with the odor of accumulated filth. Two small barred windows alone gave means of ventilation. He and the deserter were the only prisoners. The latter slept as soundly as though the morrow held nothing more momentous in his destiny than any of the days that had preceded it. Bridge was moved to kick the fellow into consciousness of his impending fate. Instead he walked to the south window to fill his lungs with the free air beyond his prison pen, and gaze sorrowfully at the star-lit sky which he should never again behold.

In a low tone Bridge crooned a snatch of the poem that he and Billy liked best:

And you, my sweet Penelope, out there somewhere
    you wait for me,
With buds of roses in your hair and kisses on your
    mouth.

Bridge's mental vision was concentrated upon the veranda of a white-walled ranchhouse to the east. He shook his head angrily.

"It's just as well," he thought. "She's not for me."

Something moved upon the ground beyond the window. Bridge became suddenly intent upon the thing. He saw it rise and resolve itself into the figure of a man, and then, in a low whisper, came a familiar voice:

"There ain't no roses in my hair, but there's a barker in my shirt, an' another at me side. Here's one of 'em. They got kisses beat a city block. How's the door o' this thing fastened?" The speaker was quite close to the window now, his face but a few inches from Bridge's.

"Billy!" ejaculated the condemned man.

"Surest thing you know; but about the door?"

"Just a heavy bar on the outside," replied Bridge.

"Easy," commented Billy, relieved. "Get ready to beat it when I open the door. I got a pony south o' town that'll have to carry double for a little way tonight."

"God bless you, Billy!" whispered Bridge, fervently.

"Lay low a few minutes," said Billy, and moved away toward the rear of the guardhouse.

A few minutes later there broke upon the night air the dismal hoot of an owl. At intervals of a few seconds it was repeated twice. The sentry before the guardhouse shifted his position and looked about, then he settled back, transferring his weight to the other foot, and resumed his bovine meditations.

The man at the rear of the guardhouse moved silently along the side of the structure until he stood within a few feet of the unsuspecting sentinel, hidden from him by the corner of the building. A heavy revolver dangled from his right hand. He held it loosely by the barrel, and waited.

For five minutes the silence of the night was unbroken, then from the east came a single shot, followed immediately by a scattering fusillade and a chorus of hoarse cries.

Billy Byrne smiled. The sentry resumed indications of quickness. From the barracks beyond the guardhouse came sharp commands and the sounds of men running. From the opposite end of the town the noise of battle welled up to ominous proportions.

Billy heard the soldiers stream from their quarters and a moment later saw them trot up the street at the double. Everyone was moving toward the opposite end of the town except the lone sentinel before the guardhouse. The moment seemed propitious for his attempt.

Billy peered around the corner of the guardhouse. Conditions were just as he had pictured they would be. The sentry stood gazing in the direction of the firing, his back toward the guardhouse door and Billy.

With a bound the American cleared the space between himself and the unsuspecting and unfortunate soldier. The butt of the heavy revolver fell, almost noiselessly, upon the back of the sentry's head, and the man sank to the ground without even a moan.

Turning to the door Billy knocked the bar from its place, the door swung in and Bridge slipped through to liberty.

"Quick!" said Billy. "Follow me," and turned at a rapid run toward the south edge of the town. He made no effort now to conceal his movements. Speed was the only essential, and the two covered the ground swiftly and openly without any attempt to take advantage of cover.

They reached Billy's horse unnoticed, and a moment later were trotting toward the west to circle the town and regain the trail to the north and safety.

To the east they heard the diminishing rifle fire of the combatants as Pesita's men fell steadily back before the defenders, and drew them away from Cuivaca in accordance with Billy's plan.

"Like takin' candy from a baby," said Billy, when the flickering lights of Cuivaca shone to the south of them, and the road ahead lay clear to the rendezvous of the brigands.

"Yes," agreed Bridge; "but what I'd like to know, Billy, is how you found out I was there."

"Penelope," said Byrne, laughing.

"Penelope!" queried Bridge. "I'm not at all sure that I follow you, Billy."

"Well, seein' as you're sittin' on behind you can't be

leadin' me," returned Billy; "but cuttin' the kid it was a skirt tipped it off to me where you was — the beautiful senorita of El Orobo Rancho, I think Jose called her. Now are you hep?"

Bridge gave an exclamation of astonishment. "God bless her!" he said. "She did that for me?"

"She sure did," Billy assured him, "an' I'll bet an iron case she's a-waitin' for you there with buds o' roses in her hair an' kisses on her mouth, you old son-of-a-gun, you." Billy laughed happily. He was happy anyway at having rescued Bridge, and the knowledge that his friend was in love and that the girl reciprocated his affection — all of which Billy assumed as the only explanation of her interest in Bridge — only added to his joy. "She ain't a greaser is she?" he asked presently.

"I should say not," replied Bridge. "She's a perfect queen from New York City; but, Billy, she's not for me. What she did was prompted by a generous heart. She couldn't care for me, Billy. Her father is a wealthy man — he could have the pick of the land — of many lands — if she cared to marry. You don't think for a minute she'd want a hobo, do you?"

"You can't most always tell," replied Billy, a trifle sadly. "I knew such a queen once who would have chosen a mucker, if he'd a-let her. You're stuck on her, ol' man?"

"I'm afraid I am, Billy," Bridge admitted; "but what's the use? Let's forget it. Oh, say, is this the horse I let you take the night you robbed the bank?"

"Yes," said Billy; "same little pony, an' a mighty well-behaved one, too. Why?"

"It's hers," said Bridge.

"An' she wants it back?"

"She didn't say so; but I'd like to get it to her some way," said Bridge.

"You ride it back when you go," suggested Billy.

"But I can't go back," said Bridge; "it was Grayson, the foreman, who made it so hot for me I had to leave. He tried to arrest me and send me to Villa."

"What for?" asked Billy.

"He didn't like me, and wanted to get rid of me." Bridge wouldn't say that his relations with Billy had brought him into trouble.

"Oh, well, I'll take it back myself then, and at the same time I'll tell Penelope what a regular fellow you are, and punch in the foreman's face for good luck."

"No, you mustn't go there. They know you now. It was some of El Orobo's men you shot up day before yesterday when you took their steers from them. They recognized the pony, and one of them had seen you in Cuivaca the night of the robbery. They would be sure to get you, Billy."

Shortly the two came in touch with the retreating Pesitistas who were riding slowly toward their mountain camp. Their pursuers had long since given up the chase, fearing that they might be being lured into the midst of a greatly superior force, and had returned to Cuivaca.

It was nearly morning when Bridge and Billy threw themselves down upon the latter's blankets, fagged.

"Well, well," murmured Billy Byrne; "li'l ol' Bridgie's found his Penelope," and fell asleep.

Chapter XIII

BARBARA AGAIN

Captain Billy Byrne rode out of the hills the following afternoon upon a pinto pony that showed the whites of its eyes in a wicked rim about the iris and kept its ears perpetually flattened backward.

At the end of a lariat trailed the Brazos pony, for Billy, laughing aside Bridge's pleas, was on his way to El Orobo Rancho to return the stolen horse to its fair owner.

At the moment of departure Pesita had asked Billy to ride by way of Jose's to instruct the old Indian that he should bear word to one Esteban that Pesita required his presence.

It is a long ride from the retreat of the Pesitistas to Jose's squalid hut, especially if one be leading an extra horse, and so it was that darkness had fallen long before Billy arrived in sight of Jose's. Dismounting some distance from the hut, Billy approached cautiously, since the world is filled with dangers for those who are beyond the law, and one may not be too careful.

Billy could see a light showing through a small window, and toward this he made his way. A short distance from Jose's is another, larger structure from which the former inhabitants had fled the wrath of Pesita. It was dark and apparently tenantless; but as a matter of fact a pair of eyes chanced at the very moment of Billy's coming to be looking out through the open doorway.

The owner turned and spoke to someone behind him.

"Jose has another visitor," he said. "Possibly this one is less harmless than the other. He comes with great caution. Let us investigate."

Three other men rose from their blankets upon the floor and joined the speaker. They were all armed, and clothed in the nondescript uniforms of Villistas. Billy's back was toward them as they sneaked from the hut in which they were intending to spend the night and crept quietly toward him.

Billy was busily engaged in peering through the little window into the interior of the old Indian's hovel. He saw an American in earnest conversation with Jose. Who could the man be? Billy did not recognize him; but presently Jose answered the question.

"It shall be done as you wish, Senor Grayson," he said.

"Ah!" thought Billy; "the foreman of El Orobo. I wonder what business he has with this old scoundrel — and at night."

What other thoughts Billy might have had upon the subject were rudely interrupted by four energetic gentlemen in his rear, who leaped upon him simultaneously and dragged him to the ground. Billy made no outcry; but he fought none the less strenuously for his freedom, and he fought after the manner of Grand

Avenue, which is not a pretty, however effective, way it may be.

But four against one when all the advantages lie with the four are heavy odds, and when Grayson and Jose ran out to investigate, and the ranch foreman added his weight to that of the others Billy was finally subdued. That each of his antagonists would carry mementos of the battle for many days was slight compensation for the loss of liberty. However, it was some.

After disarming their captive and tying his hands at his back they jerked him to his feet and examined him.

"Who are you?" asked Grayson. "What you doin' sneakin' 'round spyin' on me, eh?"

"If you wanna know who I am, bo," replied Billy, "go ask de Harlem Hurricane, an' as fer spyin' on youse, I wasn't; but from de looks I guess youse need spyin, yuh tinhorn."

A pony whinnied a short distance from the hut.

"That must be his horse," said one of the Villistas, and walked away to investigate, returning shortly after with the pinto pony and Brazos.

The moment Grayson saw the latter he gave an exclamation of understanding.

"I know him now," he said. "You've made a good catch, Sergeant. This is the fellow who robbed the bank at Cuivaca. I recognize him from the descriptions I've had of him, and the fact that he's got the Brazos pony makes it a cinch. Villa oughter promote you for this."

"Yep," interjected Billy, "he orter make youse an admiral at least; but youse ain't got me home yet, an' it'll take more'n four Dagos an' a tin-horn to do it."

"They'll get you there all right, my friend," Grayson assured him. "Now come along."

They bundled Billy into his own saddle, and shortly after the little party was winding southward along the river in the direction of El Orobo Rancho, with the intention of putting up there for the balance of the night where their prisoner could be properly secured and guarded. As they rode away from the dilapidated hut of the Indian the old man stood silhouetted against the rectangle of dim light which marked the open doorway, and shook his fist at the back of the departing ranch foreman.

"El cochino!" he cackled, and turned back into his hut.

At El Orobo Rancho Barbara walked to and fro outside the ranchhouse. Within her father sat reading beneath the rays of an oil lamp. From the quarters of the men came the strains of guitar music, and an occasional loud laugh indicated the climax of some of Eddie Shorter's famous Kansas farmer stories.

Barbara was upon the point of returning indoors when her attention was attracted by the approach of a half-dozen horsemen. They reined into the ranchyard and dismounted before the office building. Wondering a little who came so late, Barbara entered the house, mentioning casually to her father that which she had just seen.

The ranch owner, now always fearful of attack, was upon the point of investigating when Grayson rode up to the veranda and dismounted. Barbara and her father were at the door as he ascended the steps.

"Good news!" exclaimed the foreman. "I've got the bank robber, and Brazos, too. Caught the sneakin' coyote up to — up the river a bit." He had almost said "Jose's;" but caught himself in time. "Someone's been cuttin' the wire at the north side of the north pasture, an' I was ridin' up to see ef I could catch 'em at it," he explained.

"He is an American?" asked the boss.

"Looks like it; but he's got the heart of a greaser," replied Grayson. "Some of Villa's men are with me, and they're a-goin' to take him to Cuivaca tomorrow."

Neither Barbara nor her father seemed to enthuse much. To them an American was an American here in Mexico, where every hand was against their race. That at home they might have looked with disgust upon this same man did not alter their attitude here, that no American should take sides against his own people. Barbara said as much to Grayson.

"Why this fellow's one of Pesita's officers," exclaimed Grayson. "He don't deserve no sympathy from us nor from no other Americans. Pesita has sworn to kill every American that falls into his hands, and this fellow's with him to help him do it. He's a bad un."

"I can't help what he may do," insisted Barbara. "He's an American, and I for one would never be a party to his death at the hands of a Mexican, and it will mean death to him to be taken to Cuivaca."

"Well, miss," said Grayson, "you won't hev to be responsible — I'll take all the responsibility there is and welcome. I just thought you'd like to know we had him." He was addressing his employer. The latter nodded, and Grayson turned and left the room. Outside he cast a sneering laugh back over his shoulder and swung into his saddle.

In front of the men's quarters he drew rein again and shouted Eddie's name. Shorter came to the door.

"Get your six-shooter an' a rifle, an' come on over to the office. I want to see you a minute."

Eddie did as he was bid, and when he entered the little room he saw four Mexicans lolling about smoking cigarettes while Grayson stood before a chair in which sat a man with his arms tied behind his back. Grayson turned to Eddie.

"This party here is the slick un that robbed the bank, and got away on thet there Brazos pony thet miserable bookkeepin' dude giv him. The sergeant here an' his men are a-goin' to take him to Cuivaca in the mornin'. You stand guard over him 'til midnight, then they'll relieve you. They gotta get a little sleep first, though, an' I gotta get some supper. Don't stand fer no funny business now, Eddie," Grayson admonished him, and was on the point of leaving the office when a thought occurred to him. "Say, Shorter," he said, "they ain't no way of gettin' out of the little bedroom in back there except through this room. The windows are too small fer a big man to get through. I'll tell you what, we'll lock him up in there an' then you won't hev to worry none an' neither will we. You can jest spread out them Navajos there and go to sleep right plump ag'in the door, an' there won't nobody hev to relieve you all night."

"Sure," said Eddie, "leave it to me — I'll watch the slicker."

Satisfied that their prisoner was safe for the night the Villistas and Grayson departed, after seeing him safely locked in the back room.

At the mention by the foreman of his guard's names — Eddie and Shorter — Billy had studied the face of the young American cowpuncher, for the two names had aroused within his memory a tantalizing suggestion that they should be very familiar. Yet he could connect them in no way with anyone he had known in the past and he was quite sure that he never before had set eyes upon this man.

Sitting in the dark with nothing to occupy him Billy let his mind dwell upon the identity of his jailer, until, as may have happened to you, nothing in the whole world seemed equally as important as the solution of the mystery. Even his impending fate faded into nothingness by comparison with the momentous question as to where he had heard the name Eddie Shorter before.

As he sat puzzling his brain over the inconsequential matter something stirred upon the floor close to his feet, and presently he jerked back a booted foot that a rat had commenced to gnaw upon.

"Helluva place to stick a guy," mused Billy, "in wit a bunch o' man-eatin' rats. Hey!" and he turned his face toward the door. "You, Eddie! Come here!"

Eddie approached the door and listened.

"Wot do you want?" he asked. "None o' your funny business, you know. I'm from Shawnee, Kansas, I am, an' they don't come no slicker from nowhere on earth. You can't fool me."

Shawnee, Kansas! Eddie Shorter! The whole puzzle was cleared in Billy's mind in an instant.

"So you're Eddie Shorter of Shawnee, Kansas, are you?" called Billy. "Well I know your maw, Eddie, an' ef I had such a maw as you got I wouldn't be down here wastin' my time workin' alongside a lot of Dagos; but that ain't what I started out to say, which was that I want a light in here. The damned rats are tryin' to chaw off me kicks an' when they're done wit them they'll climb up after me an' old man Villa'll be sore as a pup."

"You know my maw?" asked Eddie, and there was a wistful note in his voice. "Aw shucks! you don't know her — that's jest some o' your funny, slicker business. You wanna git me in there an' then you'll try an' git aroun' me some sort o' way to let you escape; but I'm too slick for that."

"On the level Eddie, I know your maw," persisted Billy. "I ben in your maw's house jest a few weeks ago. 'Member the horsehair sofa between the windows? 'Member the Bible on the little marble-topped table? Eh? An' Tige? Well, Tige's croaked; but your maw an' your paw ain't an' they want you back, Eddie. I don't care ef you believe me, son, or not; but your maw was mighty good to me, an' you promise me you'll write her an' then go back home as fast as you can. It ain't everybody's got a swell maw like that, an' them as has ought to be good to 'em."

Beyond the closed door Eddie's jaw was commencing to tremble. Memory was flooding his heart and his eyes with sweet recollections of an ample breast where he used to pillow his head, of a big capable hand that was wont to smooth his brow and stroke back his red hair. Eddie gulped.

"You ain't joshin' me?" he asked. Billy Byrne caught the tremor in the voice.

"I ain't kiddin' you son," he said. "Wotinell do you take me fer — one o' these greasy Dagos? You an' I're Americans — I wouldn't string a home guy down here in this here Godforsaken neck o' the woods."

Billy heard the lock turn, and a moment later the door was cautiously opened revealing Eddie safely ensconced behind two six-shooters.

"That's right, Eddie," said Billy, with a laugh. "Don't you take no chances, no matter how much sob stuff I hand you, fer, I'll give it to you straight, ef I get the chanct I'll make my get-away; but I can't do it wit my flippers trussed, an' you wit a brace of gats sittin' on me. Let's have a light, Eddie. That won't do nobody any harm, an' it may discourage the rats."

Eddie backed across the office to a table where stood a small lamp. Keeping an eye through the door on his prisoner he lighted the lamp and carried it into the back room, setting it upon a commode which stood in one corner.

"You really seen maw?" he asked. "Is she well?"

"Looked well when I seen her," said Billy; "but she wants her boy back a whole lot. I guess she'd look better still ef he walked in on her some day."

"I'll do it," cried Eddie. "The minute they get money

for the pay I'll hike. Tell me your name. I'll ask her ef she remembers you when I get home. Gee! but I wish I was walkin' in the front door now."

"She never knew my name," said Billy; "but you tell her you seen the bo that mussed up the two yeggmen who rolled her an' were tryin' to croak her wit a butcher knife. I guess she ain't fergot. Me an' my pal were beatin' it — he was on the square but the dicks was after me an' she let us have money to make our get-away. She's all right, kid."

There came a knock at the outer office door. Eddie sprang back into the front room, closing and locking the door after him, just as Barbara entered.

"Eddie," she asked, "may I see the prisoner? I want to talk to him."

"You want to talk with a bank robber?" exclaimed Eddie. "Why you ain't crazy are you, Miss Barbara?"

"No, I'm not crazy; but I want to speak with him alone for just a moment, Eddie — please."

Eddie hesitated. He knew that Grayson would be angry if he let the boss's daughter into that back room alone with an outlaw and a robber, and the boss himself would probably be inclined to have Eddie drawn and quartered; but it was hard to refuse Miss Barbara anything.

"Where is he?" she asked.

Eddie jerked a thumb in the direction of the door. The key still was in the lock.

"Go to the window and look at the moon, Eddie," suggested the girl. "It's perfectly gorgeous tonight. Please, Eddie," as he still hesitated.

Eddie shook his head and moved slowly toward the window.

"There can't nobody refuse you nothin', miss," he said; "'specially when you got your heart set on it."

"That's a dear, Eddie," purred the girl, and moved

swiftly across the room to the locked door.

As she turned the key in the lock she felt a little shiver of nervous excitement run through her. "What sort of man would he be — this hardened outlaw and robber — this renegade American who had cast his lot with the avowed enemies of his own people?" she wondered.

Only her desire to learn of Bridge's fate urged her to attempt so distasteful an interview; but she dared not ask another to put the question for her, since should her complicity in Bridge's escape — provided of course that he had escaped — become known to Villa the fate of the Americans at El Orobo would be definitely sealed.

She turned the knob and pushed the door open, slowly. A man was sitting in a chair in the center of the room. His back was toward her. He was a big man. His broad shoulders loomed immense above the back of the rude chair. A shock of black hair, rumpled and tousled, covered a well-shaped head.

At the sound of the door creaking upon its hinges he turned his face in her direction, and as his eyes met hers all four went wide in surprise and incredulity.

"Billy!" she cried.

"Barbara! — you?" and Billy rose to his feet, his bound hands struggling to be free.

The girl closed the door behind her and crossed to him.

"You robbed the bank, Billy?" she asked. "It was you, after the promises you made me to live straight always — for my sake?" Her voice trembled with emotion. The man could see that she suffered, and yet he felt his own anguish, too.

"But you are married," he said. "I saw it in the papers. What do you care, now, Barbara? I'm nothing to you."

"I'm not married, Billy," she cried. "I couldn't marry

Mr. Mallory. I tried to make myself believe that I could; but at last I knew that I did not love him and never could, and I wouldn't marry a man I didn't love.

"I never dreamed that it was you here, Billy," she went on. "I came to ask you about Mr. Bridge. I wanted to know if he escaped, or if — if — oh, this awful country! They think no more of human life here than a butcher thinks of the life of the animal he dresses."

A sudden light illumined Billy's mind. Why had it not occurred to him before? This was Bridge's Penelope! The woman he loved was loved by his best friend. And she had sent a messenger to him, to Billy, to save her lover. She had come here to the office tonight to question a stranger — a man she thought an outlaw and a robber — because she could not rest without word from the man she loved. Billy stiffened. He was hurt to the bottom of his heart; but he did not blame Bridge — it was fate. Nor did he blame Barbara because she loved Bridge. Bridge was more her kind anyway. He was a college guy. Billy was only a mucker.

"Bridge got away all right," he said. "And say, he didn't have nothin' to do with pullin' off that safe crackin'. I done it myself. He didn't know I was in town an' I didn't know he was there. He's the squarest guy in the world, Bridge is. He follered me that night an' took a shot at me, thinkin' I was the robber all right but not knowin' I was me. He got my horse, an' when he found it was me, he made me take your pony an' make my get-away, fer he knew Villa's men would croak me sure if they caught me. You can't blame him fer that, can you? Him an' I were good pals — he couldn't do nothin' else. It was him that made me bring your pony back to you. It's in the corral now, I reckon. I was a-bringin' it back when they got me. Now you better go. This ain't no place fer you, an' I ain't had no sleep fer so long I'm most dead." His tones were cool. He appeared bored by her company; though as a matter of fact his heart was breaking with love for her — love that he believed unrequited — and he yearned to tear loose his bonds and crush her in his arms.

It was Barbara's turn now to be hurt. She drew herself up.

"I am sorry that I have disturbed your rest," she said, and walked away, her head in the air; but all the way back to the ranchhouse she kept repeating over and over to herself: "Tomorrow they will shoot him! Tomorrow they will shoot him! Tomorrow they will shoot him!"

Chapter XIV

'TWIXT LOVE
AND DUTY

*F*or an hour Barbara Harding paced the veranda of the ranchhouse, pride and love battling for the ascendancy within her breast. She could not let him die, that she knew; but how might she save him?

The strains of music and the laughter from the bunkhouse had ceased. The ranch slept. Over the brow of the low bluff upon the opposite side of the river a little party of silent horsemen filed downward to the ford. At the bluff's foot a barbed-wire fence marked the eastern boundary of the ranch's enclosed fields. The foremost horseman dismounted and cut the strands of wire, carrying them to one side from the path of the feet of the horses which now passed through the opening he had made.

Down into the river they rode following the ford even in the darkness with an assurance which indicated long familiarity. Then through a fringe of willows out

across a meadow toward the ranch buildings the riders
made their way. The manner of their approach, their
utter silence, the hour, all contributed toward the sinister.

Upon the veranda of the ranchhouse Barbara Harding came to a sudden halt. Her entire manner indicated
final decision, and determination. A moment she
stood in thought and then ran quickly down the steps
and in the direction of the office. Here she found Eddie
dozing at his post. She did not disturb him. A glance
through the window satisfied her that he was alone
with the prisoner. From the office building Barbara
passed on to the corral. A few horses stood within the
enclosure, their heads drooping dejectedly. As she entered they raised their muzzles and sniffed suspiciously, ears a-cock, and as the girl approached closer
to them they moved warily away, snorting, and passed
around her to the opposite side of the corral. As they
moved by her she scrutinized them and her heart
dropped, for Brazos was not among them. He must
have been turned out into the pasture.

She passed over to the bars that closed the opening
from the corral into the pasture and wormed her way
between two of them. A hackamore with a piece of
halter rope attached to it hung across the upper bar.
Taking it down she moved off across the pasture in the
direction the saddle horses most often took when
liberated from the corral.

If they had not crossed the river she felt that she
might find and catch Brazos, for lumps of sugar and
bits of bread had inspired in his equine soul a wondrous attachment for his temporary mistress.

Down the beaten trail the animals had made to the
river the girl hurried, her eyes penetrating the darkness
ahead and to either hand for the looming bulks that
would be the horses she sought, and among which she

might hope to discover the gentle little Brazos.

The nearer she came to the river the lower dropped her spirits, for as yet no sign of the animals was to be seen. To have attempted to place a hackamore upon any of the wild creatures in the corral would have been the height of foolishness — only a well-sped riata in the hands of a strong man could have captured one of these.

Closer and closer to the fringe of willows along the river she came, until, at their very edge, there broke upon her already taut nerves the hideous and uncanny scream of a wildcat. The girl stopped short in her tracks. She felt the chill of fear creep through her skin, and a twitching at the roots of her hair evidenced to her the extremity of her terror. Should she turn back? The horses might be between her and the river, but judgment told her that they had crossed. Should she brave the nervous fright of a passage through that dark, forbidding labyrinth of gloom when she knew that she should not find the horses within reach beyond?

She turned to retrace her steps. She must find another way!

But was there another way? And "Tomorrow they will shoot him!" She shuddered, bit her lower lip in an effort to command her courage, and then, wheeling, plunged into the thicket.

Again the cat screamed — close by — but the girl never hesitated in her advance, and a few moments later she broke through the willows a dozen paces from the river bank. Her eyes strained through the night; but no horses were to be seen.

The trail, cut by the hoofs of many animals, ran deep and straight down into the swirling water. Upon the opposite side Brazos must be feeding or resting, just beyond reach.

Barbara dug her nails into her palms in the bitterness

of her disappointment. She followed down to the very
edge of the water. It was black and forbidding. Even in
the daytime she would not have been confident of
following the ford — by night it would be madness to
attempt it.

She choked down a sob. Her shoulders drooped. Her
head bent forward. She was the picture of disappointment and despair.

"What can I do?" she moaned. "Tomorrow they will
shoot him!"

The thought seemed to electrify her.

"They shall not shoot him!" she cried aloud. "They
shall not shoot him while I live to prevent it!"

Again her head was up and her shoulders squared.
Tying the hackamore about her waist, she took a single
deep breath of reassurance and stepped out into the
river. For a dozen paces she found no difficulty in
following the ford. It was broad and straight; but
toward the center of the river, as she felt her way along
a step at a time, she came to a place where directly
before her the ledge upon which she crossed shelved
off into deep water. She turned upward, trying to locate
the direction of the new turn; but here too there was
no footing. Down river she felt solid rock beneath her
feet. Ah! this was the way, and boldly she stepped out,
the water already above her knees. Two, three steps she
took, and with each one her confidence and hope
arose, and then the fourth step — and there was no
footing. She felt herself lunging into the stream, and
tried to draw back and regain the ledge; but the force
of the current was too much for her, and, so suddenly
it seemed that she had thrown herself in, she was in
the channel swimming for her life.

The trend of the current there was back in the direction of the bank she had but just quitted, yet so strong
was her determination to succeed for Billy Byrne's sake

that she turned her face toward the opposite shore and fought to reach the seemingly impossible goal which love had set for her. Again and again she was swept under by the force of the current. Again and again she rose and battled, not for her own life; but for the life of the man she once had loathed and whom she later had come to love. Inch by inch she won toward the shore of her desire, and inch by inch of her progress she felt her strength failing. Could she win? Ah! if she were but a man, and with the thought came another: Thank God that I am a woman with a woman's love which gives strength to drive me into the clutches of death for his sake!

Her heart thundered in tumultuous protest against the strain of her panting lungs. Her limbs felt cold and numb; but she could not give up even though she was now convinced that she had thrown her life away uselessly. They would find her body; but no one would ever guess what had driven her to her death. Not even he would know that it was for his sake. And then she felt the tugging of the channel current suddenly lessen, an eddy carried her gently inshore, her feet touched the sand and gravel of the bottom.

Gasping for breath, staggering, stumbling, she reeled on a few paces and then slipped down clutching at the river's bank. Here the water was shallow, and here she lay until her strength returned. Then she urged herself up and onward, climbed to the top of the bank with success at last within reach.

To find the horses now required but a few minutes' search. They stood huddled in a black mass close to the barbed-wire fence at the extremity of the pasture. As she approached them they commenced to separate slowly, edging away while they faced her in curiosity. Softly she called: "Brazos! Come, Brazos!" until a unit of the moving mass detached itself and came toward her, nickering.

"Good Brazos!" she cooed. "That's a good pony," and walked forward to meet him.

The animal let her reach up and stroke his forehead, while he muzzled about her for the expected tidbit. Gently she worked the hackamore over his nose and above his ears, and when it was safely in place she breathed a deep sigh of relief and throwing her arms about his neck pressed her cheek to his.

"You dear old Brazos," she whispered.

The horse stood quietly while the girl wriggled herself to his back, and then at a word and a touch from her heels moved off at a walk in the direction of the ford. The crossing this time was one of infinite ease, for Barbara let the rope lie loose and Brazos take his own way.

Through the willows upon the opposite bank he shouldered his path, across the meadow still at a walk, lest they arouse attention, and through a gate which led directly from the meadow into the ranchyard. Here she tied him to the outside of the corral, while she went in search of saddle and bridle. Whose she took she did not know, nor care, but that the saddle was enormously heavy she was perfectly aware long before she had dragged it halfway to where Brazos stood.

Three times she essayed to lift it to his back before she succeeded in accomplishing the Herculean task, and had it been any other horse upon the ranch than Brazos the thing could never have been done; but the kindly little pony stood in statuesque resignation while the heavy Mexican tree was banged and thumped against his legs and ribs, until a lucky swing carried it to his wethers.

Saddled and bridled Barbara led him to the rear of the building and thus, by a roundabout way, to the back of the office building. Here she could see a light in the room in which Billy was confined, and after dropping the bridle reins to the ground she made her way to the front of the structure.

Creeping stealthily to the porch she peered in at the window. Eddie was stretched out in cramped though seeming luxury in an office chair. His feet were cocked up on the desk before him. In his lap lay his six-shooter ready for any emergency. Another reposed in its holster at his belt.

Barbara tiptoed to the door. Holding her breath she turned the knob gently. The door swung open without a sound, and an instant later she stood within the room. Again her eyes were fixed upon Eddie Shorter. She saw his nerveless fingers relax their hold upon the grip of his revolver. She saw the weapon slip farther down into his lap. He did not move, other than to the deep and regular breathing of profound slumber.

Barbara crossed the room to his side.

Behind the ranchhouse three figures crept forward in the shadows. Behind them a matter of a hundred yards stood a little clump of horses and with them were the figures of more men. These waited in silence. The other three crept toward the house. It was such a ranchhouse as you might find by the scores or hundreds throughout Texas. Grayson, evidently, or some other Texan, had designed it. There was nothing Mexican about it, nor anything beautiful. It stood two storied, verandaed and hideous, a blot upon the soil of picturesque Mexico.

To the roof of the veranda clambered the three prowlers, and across it to an open window. The window belonged to the bedroom of Miss Barbara Harding. Here they paused and listened, then two of them entered the room. They were gone for but a few minutes. When they emerged they showed evidences, by their gestures to the third man who had awaited outside, of disgust and disappointment.

Cautiously they descended as they had come and made their way back to those other men who had remained with the horses. Here there ensued a low-toned conference, and while it progressed Barbara Harding reached forth a steady hand which belied the terror in her soul and plucked the revolver from Eddie Shorter's lap. Eddie slept on.

Again on tiptoe the girl recrossed the office to the locked door leading into the back room. The key was in the lock. Gingerly she turned it, keeping a furtive eye upon the sleeping guard, and the muzzle of his own revolver leveled menacingly upon him. Eddie Shorter stirred in his sleep and raised a hand to his face. The heart of Barbara Harding ceased to beat while she stood waiting for the man to open his eyes and discover her; but he did nothing of the kind. Instead his hand dropped limply at his side and he resumed his regular breathing.

The key turned in the lock beneath the gentle pressure of her fingers, the bolt slipped quietly back and she pushed the door ajar. Within, Billy Byrne turned inquiring eyes in the direction of the opening door, and as he saw who it was who entered surprise showed upon his face; but he spoke no word for the girl held a silencing finger to her lips.

Quickly she came to his side and motioned him to rise while she tugged at the knots which held the bonds in place about his arms. Once she stopped long enough to recross the room and close the door which she had left open when she entered.

It required fully five minutes — the longest five minutes of Barbara Harding's life, she thought — before the knots gave to her efforts; but at last the rope fell to the floor and Billy Byrne was free.

He started to speak, to thank her, and, perhaps, to

scold her for the rash thing she had undertaken for him; but she silenced him again, and with a whispered, "Come!" turned toward the door.

As she opened it a crack to reconnoiter she kept the revolver pointed straight ahead of her into the adjoining room. Eddie, however, still slept on in peaceful ignorance of the trick which was being played upon him.

Now the two started forward for the door which opened from the office upon the porch, and as they did so Barbara turned again toward Billy to caution him to silence for his spurs had tinkled as he moved. For a moment their eyes were not upon Eddie Shorter and Fate had it that at that very moment Eddie awoke and opened his own eyes.

The sight that met them was so astonishing that for a second the Kansan could not move. He saw Barbara Harding, a revolver in her hand, aiding the outlaw to escape, and in the instant that surprise kept him motionless Eddie saw, too, another picture — the picture of a motherly woman in a little farmhouse back in Kansas, and Eddie realized that this man, this outlaw, had been the means of arousing within him a desire and a determination to return again to those loving arms. Too, the man had saved his mother from injury, and possible death.

Eddie shut his eyes quickly and thought hard and fast. Miss Barbara had always been kind to him. In his boyish heart he had loved her, hopelessly of course, in a boyish way. She wanted the outlaw to escape. Eddie realized that he would do anything that Miss Barbara wanted, even if he had to risk his life at it.

The girl and the man were at the door. She pushed him through ahead of her while she kept the revolver leveled upon Eddie, then she passed out after him and closed the door, while Eddie Shorter kept his eyes tightly closed and prayed to his God that Billy Byrne might get safely away.

Outside and in the rear of the office building Barbara pressed the revolver upon Billy.

"You will need it," she said. "There is Brazos — take him. God bless and guard you, Billy!" and she was gone.

Billy swallowed bard. He wanted to run after her and take her in his arms; but he recalled Bridge, and with a sigh turned toward the patient Brazos. Languidly he gathered up the reins and mounted, and then unconcernedly as though he were an honored guest departing by daylight he rode out of the ranchyard and turned Brazos' head north up the river road.

And as Billy disappeared in the darkness toward the north Barbara Harding walked slowly toward the ranchhouse, while from a little group of men and horses a hundred yards away three men detached themselves and crept toward her, for they had seen her in the moonlight as she left Billy outside the office and strolled slowly in the direction of the house.

They hid in the shadow at the side of the house until the girl had turned the corner and was approaching the veranda, then they ran quickly forward and as she mounted the steps she was seized from behind and dragged backward. A hand was clapped over her mouth and a whispered threat warned her to silence.

Half dragging and half carrying her the three men bore her back to where their confederates awaited them. A huge fellow mounted his pony and Barbara was lifted to the horn of the saddle before him. Then the others mounted and as silently as they had come they rode away, following the same path.

Barbara Harding had not cried out nor attempted to, for she had seen very shortly after her capture that she was in the hands of Indians and she judged from what she had heard of the little band of Pimans who held forth in the mountains to the east that they would as gladly knife her as not.

Jose was a Piman, and she immediately connected Jose with the perpetration, or at least the planning of her abduction. Thus she felt assured that no harm would come to her, since Jose had been famous in his time for the number and size of the ransoms he had collected.

Her father would pay what was demanded, she would be returned and, aside from a few days of discomfort and hardship, she would be none the worse off for her experience. Reasoning thus it was not difficult to maintain her composure and presence of mind.

As Barbara was borne toward the east, Billy Byrne rode steadily northward. It was his intention to stop at Jose's hut and deliver the message which Pesita had given him for the old Indian. Then he would disappear into the mountains to the west, join Pesita and urge a new raid upon some favored friend of General Francisco Villa, for Billy had no love for Villa.

He should have been glad to pay his respects to El Orobo Rancho and its foreman; but the fact that Anthony Harding owned it and that he and Barbara were there was sufficient effectually to banish all thoughts of revenge along that line.

"Maybe I can get his goat later," he thought, "when he's away from the ranch. I don't like that stiff, anyhow. He orter been a harness bull."

It was four o'clock in the morning when Billy dismounted in front of Jose's hut. He pounded on the door until the man came and opened it.

"Eh!" exclaimed Jose as he saw who his early morning visitor was, "you got away from them. Fine!" and the old man chuckled. "I send word to Pesita two, four hours ago that Villistas capture Capitan Byrne and take him to Cuivaca."

"Thanks," said Billy. "Pesita wants you to send Esteban to him. I didn't have no chance to tell you last night while them pikers was stickin' aroun', so I stops now on my way back to the hills."

"I will send Esteban tonight if I can get him; but I do not know. Esteban is working for the pig, Grayson."

"Wot's he doin' fer Grayson?" asked Billy. "And what was the Grayson guy doin' up here with you, Jose? Ain't you gettin' pretty thick with Pesita's enemies?"

"Jose good friends everybody," and the old man grinned. "Grayson have a job he want good men for. Jose furnish men. Grayson pay well. Job got nothin' do Pesita, Villa, Carranza, revolution — just private job. Grayson want senorita. He pay to get her. That all."

"Oh," said Billy, and yawned. He was not interested in Mr. Grayson's amours. "Why didn't the poor boob go get her himself?" he inquired disinterestedly. "He must be a yap to hire a bunch o' guys to go cop off a siwash girl fer him."

"It is not a siwash girl, Senor Capitan," said Jose. "It is one beautiful senorita — the daughter of the owner of El Orobo Rancho."

"What?" cried Billy Byrne. "What's that you say?"

"Yes, Senor Capitan, what of it?" inquired Jose. "Grayson he pay me furnish the men. Esteban he go with his warriors. I get Esteban. They go tonight take away the senorita; but not for Grayson," and the old fellow laughed. "I can no help can I? Grayson pay me money get men. I get them. I no help if they keep girl," and he shrugged.

"They're comin' for her tonight?" cried Billy.

"Si, senor," replied Jose. "Doubtless they already take her."

"Hell!" muttered Billy Byrne, as he swung Brazos

about so quickly that the little pony pivoted upon his hind legs and dashed away toward the south over the same trail he had just traversed.

Chapter XV

AN INDIAN'S TREACHERY

*T*he Brazos pony had traveled far that day but for only a trifle over ten miles had he carried a rider upon his back. He was, consequently, far from fagged as he leaped forward to the lifted reins and tore along the dusty river trail back in the direction of Orobo.

Never before had Brazos covered ten miles in so short a time, for it was not yet five o'clock when, reeling with fatigue, he stopped, staggered and fell in front of the office building at El Orobo.

Eddie Shorter had sat in the chair as Barbara and Billy had last seen him waiting until Byrne should have an ample start before arousing Grayson and reporting the prisoner's escape. Eddie had determined that he would give Billy an hour. He grinned as he anticipated the rage of Grayson and the Villistas when they learned that their bird had flown, and as he mused and waited he fell asleep.

It was broad daylight when Eddie awoke, and as he looked up at the little clock ticking against the wall, and saw the time he gave an exclamation of surprise and leaped to his feet. Just as he opened the outer door of the office he saw a horseman leap from a winded pony in front of the building. He saw the animal collapse and sink to the ground, and then he recognized the pony as Brazos, and another glance at the man brought recognition of him, too.

"You?" cried Eddie. "What are you doin' back here? I gotta take you now," and he started to draw his revolver; but Billy Byrne had him covered before ever his hand reached the grip of his gun.

"Put 'em up!" admonished Billy, "and listen to me. This ain't no time fer gunplay or no such foolishness. I ain't back here to be took — get that out o' your nut. I'm tipped off that a bunch o' siwashes was down here last night to swipe Miss Harding. Come! We gotta go see if she's here or not, an' don't try any funny business on me, Eddie. I ain't a-goin' to be taken again, an' whoever tries it gets his, see?"

Eddie was down off the porch in an instant, and making for the ranchhouse.

"I'm with you," he said. "Who told you? And who done it?"

"Never mind who told me; but a siwash named Esteban was to pull the thing off for Grayson. Grayson wanted Miss Harding an' he was goin' to have her stolen for him."

"The hound!" muttered Eddie.

The two men dashed up onto the veranda of the ranchhouse and pounded at the door until a Chinaman opened it and stuck out his head, inquiringly.

"Is Miss Harding here?" demanded Billy.

"Mlissy Hardie Kleep," snapped the servant. "Wally wanee here flo blekfas?," and would have shut the door in their faces had not Billy intruded a heavy boot. The next instant he placed a large palm over the celestial's face and pushed the man back into the house. Once inside he called Mr. Harding's name aloud.

"What is it?" asked the gentleman a moment later as he appeared in a bedroom doorway off the living-room clad in his pajamas. "What's the matter? Why, gad man, is that you? Is this really Billy Byrne?"

"Sure," replied Byrne shortly; "but we can't waste any time chinnin'. I heard that Miss Barbara was goin' to be swiped last night — I heard that she had been. Now hurry and see if she is here."

Anthony Harding turned and leaped up the narrow stairway to the second floor four steps at a time. He hadn't gone upstairs in that fashion in forty years. Without even pausing to rap he burst into his daughter's bedroom. It was empty. The bed was unruffled. It had not been slept in. With a moan the man turned back and ran hastily to the other rooms upon the second floor — Barbara was nowhere to be found. Then he hastened downstairs to the two men awaiting him.

As he entered the room from one end Grayson entered it from the other through the doorway leading out upon the veranda. Billy Byrne had heard footsteps upon the boards without and he was ready, so that as Grayson entered he found himself looking straight at the business end of a sixshooter. The foreman halted, and stood looking in surprise first at Billy Byrne, and then at Eddie Shorter and Mr. Harding.

"What does this mean?" he demanded, addressing Eddie. "What you doin' here with your prisoner? Who told you to let him out, eh?"

"Can the chatter," growled Billy Byrne. "Shorter didn't let me out. I escaped hours ago, and I've just come back from Jose's to ask you where Miss Harding is, you low-lived cur, you. Where is she?"

"What has Mr. Grayson to do with it?" asked Mr. Harding. "How should he know anything about it? It's all a mystery to me — you here, of all men in the world, and Grayson talking about you as the prisoner. I can't make it out. Quick, though, Byrne, tell me all you know about Barbara."

Billy kept Grayson covered as he replied to the request of Harding.

"This guy hires a bunch of Pimans to steal Miss Barbara," he said. "I got it straight from the fellow he paid the money to for gettin' him the right men to pull off the job. He wants her it seems," and Billy shot a look at the ranch foreman that would have killed if looks could. "She can't have been gone long. I seen her after midnight, just before I made my getaway, so they can't have taken her very far. This thing here can't help us none neither, for he don't know where she is any more'n we do. He thinks he does; but he don't. The siwashes framed it on him, an' they've doubled-crossed him. I got that straight too; but, Gawd! I don't know where they've taken her or what they're goin' to do with her."

As he spoke he turned his eyes for the first time away from Grayson and looked full in Anthony Harding's face. The latter saw beneath the strong character lines of the other's countenance the agony of fear and doubt that lay heavy upon his heart.

In the brief instant that Billy's watchful gaze left the figure of the ranch foreman the latter saw the opportunity he craved. He was standing directly in the doorway — a single step would carry him out of range of Byrne's gun, placing a wall between it and him, and Grayson was not slow in taking that step.

When Billy turned his eyes back the Texan had disappeared, and by the time the former reached the doorway Grayson was halfway to the office building on the veranda of which stood the four soldiers of Villa grumbling and muttering over the absence of their prisoner of the previous evening.

Billy Byrne stepped out into the open. The ranch foreman called aloud to the four Mexicans that their prisoner was at the ranchhouse and as they looked in that direction they saw him, revolver in hand, coming slowly toward them. There was a smile upon his lips which they could not see because of the distance, and which, not knowing Billy Byrne, they would not have interpreted correctly; but the revolver they did understand, and at sight of it one of them threw his carbine to his shoulder. His finger, however, never closed upon the trigger, for there came the sound of a shot from beyond Billy Byrne and the Mexican staggered forward, pitching over the edge of the porch to the ground.

Billy turned his head in the direction from which the shot had come and saw Eddie Shorter running toward him, a smoking six-shooter in his right hand.

"Go back," commanded Byrne; "this is my funeral."

"Not on your life," replied Eddie Shorter. "Those greasers don't take no white man off'n El Orobo, while I'm here. Get busy! They're comin'."

And sure enough they were coming, and as they came their carbines popped and the bullets whizzed about the heads of the two Americans. Grayson, too, had taken a hand upon the side of the Villistas. From the bunkhouse other men were running rapidly in the direction of the fight, attracted by the first shots.

Billy and Eddie stood their ground, a few paces apart. Two more of Villa's men went down. Grayson ran for cover. Then Billy Byrne dropped the last of the Mexicans just as the men from the bunkhouse came panting upon the scene. There were both Americans and Mexicans among them. All were armed and weapons were ready in their hands.

They paused a short distance from the two men. Eddie's presence upon the side of the stranger saved

Billy from instant death, for Eddie was well liked by both his Mexican and American fellow-workers.

"What's the fuss?" asked an American.

Eddie told them, and when they learned that the boss's daughter had been spirited away and that the ranch foreman was at the bottom of it the anger of the Americans rose to a dangerous pitch.

"Where is he?" someone asked. They were gathered in a little cluster now about Billy Byrne and Shorter.

"I saw him duck behind the office building," said Eddie.

"Come on," said another. "We'll get him."

"Someone get a rope." The men spoke in low, ordinary tones — they appeared unexcited. Determination was the most apparent characteristic of the group. One of them ran back toward the bunkhouse for his rope. The others walked slowly in the direction of the rear of the office building. Grayson was not there. The search proceeded. The Americans were in advance. The Mexicans kept in a group by themselves a little in rear of the others — it was not their trouble. If the gringos wanted to lynch another gringo, well and good — that was the gringos' business. They would keep out of it, and they did.

Down past the bunkhouse and the cookhouse to the stables the searchers made their way. Grayson could not be found. In the stables one of the men made a discovery — the foreman's saddle had vanished. Out in the corrals they went. One of the men laughed — the bars were down and the saddle horses gone. Eddie Shorter presently pointed out across the pasture and the river to the skyline of the low bluffs beyond. The others looked. A horseman was just visible urging his mount upward to the crest, the two stood in silhouette against the morning sky pink with the new sun.

"That's him," said Eddie.

"Let him go," said Billy Byrne. "He won't never come back and he ain't worth chasin'. Not while we got Miss Barbara to look after. My horse is down there with yours. I'm goin' down to get him. Will you come, Shorter? I may need help — I ain't much with a rope yet."

He started off without waiting for a reply, and all the Americans followed. Together they circled the horses and drove them back to the corral. When Billy had saddled and mounted he saw that the others had done likewise.

"We're goin' with you," said one of the men. "Miss Barbara b'longs to us."

Billy nodded and moved off in the direction of the ranchhouse. Here he dismounted and with Eddie Shorter and Mr. Harding commenced circling the house in search of some manner of clue to the direction taken by the abductors. It was not long before they came upon the spot where the Indians' horses had stood the night before. From there the trail led plainly down toward the river. In a moment ten Americans were following it, after Mr. Harding had supplied Billy Byrne with a carbine, another six-shooter, and ammunition.

Through the river and the cut in the barbed-wire fence, then up the face of the bluff and out across the low mesa beyond the trail led. For a mile it was distinct, and then disappeared as though the riders had separated.

"Well," said Billy, as the others drew around him for consultation, "they'd be goin' to the hills there. They was Pimans — Esteban's tribe. They got her up there in the hills somewheres. Let's split up an' search the hills for her. Whoever comes on 'em first'll have to do some shootin' and the rest of us can close in an' help. We can go in pairs — then if one's killed the other can ride out an' lead the way back to where it happened."

The men seemed satisfied with the plan and broke up into parties of two. Eddie Shorter paired off with Billy Byrne.

"Spread out," said the latter to his companions. "Eddie an' I'll ride straight ahead — the rest of you can fan out a few miles on either side of us. S'long an' good luck," and he started off toward the hills, Eddie Shorter at his side.

Back at the ranch the Mexican vaqueros lounged about, grumbling. With no foreman there was nothing to do except talk about their troubles. They had not been paid since the looting of the bank at Cuivaca, for Mr. Harding had been unable to get any silver from elsewhere until a few days since. He now had assurances that it was on the way to him; but whether or not it would reach El Orobo was a question.

"Why should we stay here when we are not paid?" asked one of them.

"Yes, why?" chorused several others.

"There is nothing to do here," said another. "We will go to Cuivaca. I, for one, am tired of working for the gringos."

This met with the unqualified approval of all, and a few moments later the men had saddled their ponies and were galloping away in the direction of sun-baked Cuivaca. They sang now, and were happy, for they were as little boys playing hooky from school — not bad men; but rather irresponsible children.

Once in Cuivaca they swooped down upon the drinking-place, where, with what little money a few of them had left they proceeded to get drunk.

Later in the day an old, dried-up Indian entered. He was hot and dusty from a long ride.

"Hey, Jose!" cried one of the vaqueros from El Orobo Rancho; "you old rascal, what are you doing here?"

Jose looked around upon them. He knew them all — they represented the Mexican contingent of the riders of El Orobo. Jose wondered what they were all doing here in Cuivaca at one time. Even upon a pay day it never had been the rule of El Orobo to allow more than four men at a time to come to town.

"Oh, Jose come to buy coffee and tobacco," he replied. He looked about searchingly. "Where are the others?" he asked, "— the gringos?"

"They have ridden after Esteban," explained one of the vaqueros. "He has run off with Senorita Harding."

Jose raised his eyebrows as though this was all news.

"And Senor Grayson has gone with them?" he asked. "He was very fond of the senorita."

"Senor Grayson has run away," went on the other speaker. "The other gringos wished to hang him, for it is said he has bribed Esteban to do this thing."

Again Jose raised his eyebrows. "Impossible!" he ejaculated. "And who then guards the ranch?" he asked presently.

"Senor Harding, two Mexican house servants, and a Chinaman," and the vaquero laughed.

"I must be going," Jose announced after a moment. "It is a long ride for an old man from my poor home to Cuivaca, and back again."

The vaqueros were paying no further attention to him, and the Indian passed out and sought his pony; but when he had mounted and ridden from town he took a strange direction for one whose path lies to the east, since he turned his pony's head toward the north-west.

Jose had ridden far that day, since Billy had left his humble hut. He had gone to the west to the little rancho of one of Pesita's adherents who had dispatched a boy to carry word to the bandit that his Captain Byrne had escaped the Villistas, and then Jose had ridden into Cuivaca by a circuitous route which brought him up from the east side of the town.

Now he was riding once again for Pesita; but this time he would bear the information himself. He found the chief in camp and after begging tobacco and a cigarette paper the Indian finally reached the purpose of his visit.

"Jose has just come from Cuivaca," he said, "and there he drank with all the Mexican vaqueros of El Orobo Rancho — *all*, my general, you understand. It seems that Esteban has carried off the beautiful senorita of El Orobo Rancho, and the vaqueros tell Jose that *all* the American vaqueros have ridden in search of her — *all*, my general, you understand. In such times of danger it is odd that the gringos should leave El Orobo thus unguarded. Only the rich Senor Harding, two house servants, and a Chinaman remain."

A man lay stretched upon his blankets in a tent next to that occupied by Pesita. At the sound of the speaker's voice, low though it was, he raised his head and listened. He heard every word, and a scowl settled upon his brow. Barbara stolen! Mr. Harding practically alone upon the ranch! And Pesita in possession of this information!

Bridge rose to his feet. He buckled his cartridge belt about his waist and picked up his carbine, then he crawled under the rear wall of his tent and walked slowly off in the direction of the picket line where the horses were tethered.

"Ah, Senor Bridge," said a pleasant voice in his ear; "where to?"

Bridge turned quickly to look into the smiling, evil face of Rozales.

"Oh," he replied, "I'm going out to see if I can't find some shooting. It's awfully dull sitting around here doing nothing."

"Si, senor," agreed Rozales; "I, too, find it so. Let us go together — I know where the shooting is best."

"I don't doubt it," thought Bridge; "probably in the back;" but aloud he said: "Certainly, that will be fine," for he guessed that Rozales had been set to watch his movements and prevent his escape, and, perchance, to be the sole witness of some unhappy event which should carry Senor Bridge to the arms of his fathers.

Rozales called a soldier to saddle and bridle their horses and shortly after the two were riding abreast down the trail out of the hills. Where it was necessary that they ride in single file Bridge was careful to see that Rozales rode ahead, and the Mexican graciously permitted the American to fall behind.

If he was inspired by any other motive than simple espionage he was evidently content to bide his time until chance gave him the opening he desired, and it was equally evident that he felt as safe in front of the American as behind him.

At a point where a ravine down which they had ridden debauched upon a mesa Rozales suggested that they ride to the north, which was not at all the direction in which Bridge intended going. The American de-murred.

"But there is no shooting down in the valley," urged Rozales.

"I think there will be," was Bridge's enigmatical reply, and then, with a sudden exclamation of surprise he pointed over Rozales' shoulder. "What's that?" he cried in a voice tense with excitement.

The Mexican turned his head quickly in the direction Bridge's index finger indicated.

"I see nothing," said Rozales, after a moment.

"You do now, though," replied Bridge, and as the Mexican's eyes returned in the direction of his com-panion he was forced to admit that he did see something — the dismal, hollow eye of a six-shooter looking him straight in the face.

"Senor Bridge!" exclaimed Rozales. "What are you doing? What do you mean?"

"I mean," said Bridge, "that if you are at all solicitous of your health you'll climb down off that pony, not forgetting to keep your hands above your head when you reach the ground. Now climb!"

Rozales dismounted.

"Turn your back toward me," commanded the American, and when the other had obeyed him, Bridge dismounted and removed the man's weapons from his belt. "Now you may go, Rozales," he said, "and should you ever have an American in your power again remember that I spared your life when I might easily have taken it — when it would have been infinitely safer for me to have done it."

The Mexican made no reply, but the black scowl that clouded his face boded ill for the next gringo who should be so unfortunate as to fall into his hands. Slowly he wheeled about and started back up the trail in the direction of the Pesita camp.

"I'll be halfway to El Orobo," thought Bridge, "before he gets a chance to tell Pesita what happened to him," and then be remounted and rode on down into the valley, leading Rozales' horse behind him.

It would never do, he knew, to turn the animal loose too soon, since he would doubtless make his way back to camp, and in doing so would have to pass Rozales who would catch him. Time was what Bridge wanted — to be well on his way to Orobo before Pesita should learn of his escape.

Bridge knew nothing of what had happened to Billy, for Pesita had seen to it that the information was kept from the American. The latter had, nevertheless, been worrying not a little at the absence of his friend for he knew that he had taken his liberty and his life in his hands in riding down to El Orobo among avowed enemies.

Far to his rear Rozales plodded sullenly up the steep trail through the mountains, revolving in his mind various exquisite tortures he should be delighted to inflict upon the next gringo who came into his power.

Chapter XVI

EDDIE MAKES GOOD

*B*illy Byrne and Eddie Shorter rode steadily in the direction of the hills. Upon either side and at intervals of a mile or more stretched the others of their party, occasionally visible; but for the most part not. Once in the hills the two could no longer see their friends or be seen by them.

Both Byrne and Eddie felt that chance had placed them upon the right trail for a well-marked and long-used path wound upward through a canyon along which they rode. It was an excellent location for an ambush, and both men breathed more freely when they had passed out of it into more open country upon a narrow tableland between the first foothills and the main range of mountains.

Here again was the trail well marked, and when Eddie, looking ahead, saw that it appeared to lead in the direction of a vivid green spot close to the base of the gray brown hills he gave an exclamation of assurance.

"We're on the right trail all right, old man," he said. "They's water there," and he pointed ahead at the green splotch upon the gray. "That's where they'd be havin' their village. I ain't never been up here so I ain't familiar with the country. You see we don't run no cattle this side the river — the Pimans won't let us. They don't care to have no white men pokin' round in their country; but I'll bet a hat we find a camp there."

Onward they rode toward the little spot of green. Sometimes it was in sight and again as they approached higher ground, or wound through gullies and ravines it was lost to their sight; but always they kept it as their goal. The trail they were upon led to it — of that there could be no longer the slightest doubt. And as they rode with their destination in view black, beady eyes looked down upon them from the very green oasis toward which they urged their ponies — tiring now from the climb.

A lithe, brown body lay stretched comfortably upon a bed of grasses at the edge of a little rise of ground beneath which the riders must pass before they came to the cluster of huts which squatted in a tiny natural park at the foot of the main peak. Far above the watcher a spring of clear, pure water bubbled out of the mountain-side, and running downward formed little pools among the rocks which held it. And with this water the Pimans irrigated their small fields before it sank from sight again into the earth just below their village. Beside the brown body lay a long rifle. The man's eyes watched, unblinking, the two specks far below him whom he knew and had known for an hour were gringos.

Another brown body wormed itself forward to his side and peered over the edge of the declivity down upon the white men. He spoke a few words in a whisper to him who watched with the rifle, and then crawled back again and disappeared. And all the while, onward and upward came Billy Byrne and Eddie Shorter, each knowing in his heart that if not already, then at any moment a watcher would discover them and a little later a bullet would fly that would find one of them, and they took the chance for the sake of the American girl who lay hidden somewhere in these hills, for in no other way could they locate her hiding place more quickly. Any one of the other eight Americans who rode in pairs into the hills at other points to the left and right of Billy Byrne and his companion would have and was even then cheerfully taking the same chances that Eddie and Billy took, only the latter were now assured that to one of them would fall the sacrifice, for as they had come closer Eddie had seen a thin wreath of smoke rising from among the trees of the oasis. Now, indeed, were they sure that they had chanced upon the trail to the Piman village.

"We gotta keep our eyes peeled," said Eddie, as they wound into a ravine which from its location evidently led directly up to the village. "We ain't far from 'em now, an' if they get us they'll get us about here."

As though to punctuate his speech with the final period a rifle cracked above them. Eddie jumped spasmodically and clutched his breast.

"I'm hit," he said, quite unemotionally.

Billy Byrne's revolver had answered the shot from above them, the bullet striking where Billy had seen a puff of smoke following the rifle shot. Then Billy turned toward Eddie.

"Hit bad?" he asked.

"Yep, I guess so," said Eddie. "What'll we do? Hide up here, or ride back after the others?"

Another shot rang out above them, although Billy had been watching for a target at which to shoot again — a target which he had been positive he would get when the man rose to fire again. And Billy did see the fellow at last — a few paces from where he had first fired; but not until the other had dropped Eddie's horse beneath him. Byrne fired again, and this time he had the satisfaction of seeing a brown body rise, struggle a moment, and then roll over once upon the grass before it came to rest.

"I reckon we'll stay here," said Billy, looking ruefully at Eddie's horse.

Eddie rose and as he did so he staggered and grew very white. Billy dismounted and ran forward, putting an arm about him. Another shot came from above and Billy Byrne's pony grunted and collapsed.

"Hell!" exclaimed Byrne. "We gotta get out of this," and lifting his wounded comrade in his arms he ran for the shelter of the bluff from the summit of which the snipers had fired upon them. Close in, hugging the face of the perpendicular wall of tumbled rock and earth, they were out of range of the Indians; but Billy did not stop when he had reached temporary safety. Farther up toward the direction in which lay the village, and halfway up the side of the bluff Billy saw what he took to be excellent shelter. Here the face of the bluff was less steep and upon it lay a number of large bowlders, while others protruded from the ground about them.

Toward these Billy made his way. The wounded man across his shoulder was suffering indescribable agonies; but he bit his lip and stifled the cries that each step his comrade took seemed to wrench from him, lest he attract the enemy to their position.

Above them all was silence, yet Billy knew that alert, red foemen were creeping to the edge of the bluff in search of their prey. If he could but reach the shelter of the bowlders before the Pimans discovered them!

The minutes that were consumed in covering the

hundred yards seemed as many hours to Billy Byrne; but at last he dragged the fainting cowboy between two large bowlders close under the edge of the bluff and found himself in a little, natural fortress, well adapted to defense.

From above they were protected from the fire of the Indians upon the bluff by the height of the bowlder at the foot of which they lay, while another just in front hid them from possible marksmen across the canyon. Smaller rocks scattered about gave promise of shelter from flank fire, and as soon as he had deposited Eddie in the comparative safety of their retreat Byrne commenced forming a low breastwork upon the side facing the village — the direction from which they might naturally expect attack. This done he turned his attention to the opening upon the opposite side and soon had a similar defense constructed there, then he turned his attention to Eddie, though keeping a watchful eye upon both approaches to their stronghold.

The Kansan lay upon his side, moaning. Blood stained his lips and nostrils, and when Billy Byrne opened his shirt and found a gaping wound in his right breast he knew how serious was his companion's injury. As he felt Billy working over him the boy opened his eyes.

"Do you think I'm done for?" he asked in a tortured whisper.

"Nothin' doin'," lied Billy cheerfully. "Just a scratch. You'll be all right in a day or two."

Eddie shook his head wearily. "I wish I could believe you," he said. "I ben figgerin' on goin' back to see maw. I ain't thought o' nothin' else since you told me 'bout how she missed me. I ken see her right now just like I was there. I'll bet she's scrubbin' the kitchen floor. Maw was always a-scrubbin' somethin'. Gee! but it's tough to cash in like this just when I was figgerin' on goin' home."

Billy couldn't think of anything to say. He turned to look up and down the canyon in search of the enemy.

"Home!" whispered Eddie. "Home!"

"Aw, shucks!" said Billy kindly. "You'll get home all right, kid. The boys must a-heard the shootin' an' they'll be along in no time now. Then we'll clean up this bunch o' coons an' have you back to El Orobo an' nursed into shape in no time."

Eddie tried to smile as he looked up into the other's face. He reached a hand out and laid it on Billy's arm.

"You're all right, old man," he whispered. "I know you're lyin' an' so do you; but it makes me feel better anyway to have you say them things."

Billy felt as one who has been caught stealing from a blind man. The only adequate reply of which he could think was, "Aw, shucks!"

"Say," said Eddie after a moment's silence, "if you get out o' here an' ever go back to the States promise me you'll look up maw and paw an' tell 'em I was comin' home — to stay. Tell 'em I died decent, too, will you — died like paw was always a-tellin' me my grand-dad died, fightin' Injuns 'round Fort Dodge some-wheres."

"Sure," said Billy; "I'll tell 'em. Gee! Look who's comin' here," and as he spoke he flattened himself to the ground just as a bullet pinged against the rock above his head and the report of a rifle sounded from up the canyon. "That guy most got me. I'll have to be 'tendin' to business better'n this."

He drew himself slowly up upon his elbows, his carbine ready in his hand, and peered through a small aperture between two of the rocks which composed his breastwork. Then he stuck the muzzle of the weapon through, took aim and pulled the trigger.

"Didje get him?" asked Eddie.

"Yep," said Billy, and fired again. "Got that one too. Say, they're tough-lookin' guys; but I guess they won't come so fast next time. Those two were right in the open, workin' up to us on their bellies. They must a-thought we was sleepin'."

For an hour Billy neither saw nor heard any sign of the enemy, though several times be raised his hat above the breastwork upon the muzzle of his carbine to draw their fire.

It was midafternoon when the sound of distant rifle fire came faintly to the ears of the two men from somewhere far below them.

"The boys must be comin'," whispered Eddie Shorter hopefully.

For half an hour the firing continued and then silence again fell upon the mountains. Eddie began to wander mentally. He talked much of Kansas and his old home, and many times he begged for water.

"Buck up, kid," said Billy; "the boys'll be along in a minute now an' then we'll get you all the water you want."

But the boys did not come. Billy was standing up now, stretching his legs, and searching up and down the canyon for Indians. He was wondering if he could chance making a break for the valley where they stood some slight chance of meeting with their companions, and even as he considered the matter seriously there came a staccato report and Billy Byrne fell forward in a heap.

"God!" cried Eddie. "They got him now, they got him."

Byrne stirred and struggled to rise.

"Like'll they got me," he said, and staggered to his knees.

Over the breastwork he saw a half-dozen Indians

running rapidly toward the shelter — he saw them in a haze of red that was caused not by blood but by anger. With an oath Billy Byrne leaped to his feet. From his knees up his whole body was exposed to the enemy; but Billy cared not. He was in a berserker rage. Whipping his carbine to his shoulder he let drive at the advancing Indians who were now beyond hope of cover. They must come on or be shot down where they were, so they came on, yelling like devils and stopping momentarily to fire upon the rash white man who stood so perfect a target before them.

But their haste spoiled their marksmanship. The bullets zinged and zipped against the rocky little fortress, they nicked Billy's shirt and trousers and hat, and all the while he stood there pumping lead into his assailants — not hysterically; but with the cool deliberation of a butcher slaughtering beeves.

One by one the Pimans dropped until but a single Indian rushed frantically upon the white man, and then the last of the assailants lunged forward across the breastwork with a bullet from Billy's carbine through his forehead.

Eddie Shorter had raised himself painfully upon an elbow that he might witness the battle, and when it was over he sank back, the blood welling from between his set teeth.

Billy turned to look at him when the last of the Pimans was disposed of, and seeing his condition kneeled beside him and took his head in the hollow of an arm.

"You orter lie still," he cautioned the Kansan. "'Tain't good for you to move around much."

"It was worth it," whispered Eddie. "Say, but that was some scrap. You got your nerve standin' up there against the bunch of 'em; but if you hadn't they'd have rushed us and some of 'em would a-got in."

"Funny the boys don't come," said Billy.

"Yes," replied Eddie, with a sigh; "it's milkin' time now, an' I figgered on goin' to Shawnee this evenin'. Them's nice cookies, maw. I —"

Billy Byrne was bending low to catch his feeble words, and when the voice trailed out into nothingness he lowered the tousled red head to the hard earth and turned away.

Could it be that the thing which glistened on the eyelid of the toughest guy on the West Side was a tear?

The afternoon waned and night came, but it brought to Billy Byrne neither renewed attack nor succor. The bullet which had dropped him momentarily had but creased his forehead. Aside from the fact that he was blood covered from the wound it had inconvenienced him in no way, and now that darkness had fallen he commenced to plan upon leaving the shelter.

First he transferred Eddie's ammunition to his own person, and such valuables and trinkets as he thought "maw" might be glad to have, then he removed the breechblock from Eddie's carbine and stuck it in his pocket that the weapon might be valueless to the Indians when they found it.

"Sorry I can't bury you old man," was Billy's parting comment, as he climbed over the breastwork and melted into the night.

Billy Byrne moved cautiously through the darkness, and he moved not in the direction of escape and safety but directly up the canyon in the way that the village of the Pimans lay.

Soon he heard the sound of voices and shortly after saw the light of cook fires playing upon bronzed faces and upon the fronts of low huts. Some women were moaning and wailing. Billy guessed that they mourned for those whom his bullets had found earlier in the day. In the darkness of the night, far up among the rough, forbidding mountains it was all very weird and uncanny.

Billy crept closer to the village. Shelter was abundant. He saw no sign of sentry and wondered why they should be so lax in the face of almost certain attack. Then it occurred to him that possibly the firing he and Eddie had heard earlier in the day far down among the foothills might have meant the extermination of the Americans from El Orobo.

"Well, I'll be next then," mused Billy, and wormed closer to the huts. His eyes were on the alert every instant, as were his ears; but no sign of that which he sought rewarded his keenest observation.

Until midnight he lay in concealment and all that time the mourners continued their dismal wailing. Then, one by one, they entered their huts, and silence reigned within the village.

Billy crept closer. He eyed each hut with longing, wondering gaze. Which could it be? How could he determine? One seemed little more promising than the others. He had noted those to which Indians had retired. There were three into which he had seen none go. These, then, should be the first to undergo his scrutiny.

The night was dark. The moon had not yet risen. Only a few dying fires cast a wavering and uncertain light upon the scene. Through the shadows Billy Byrne crept closer and closer. At last he lay close beside one of the huts which was to be the first to claim his attention.

For several moments he lay listening intently for any sound which might come from within; but there was none. He crawled to the doorway and peered within. Utter darkness shrouded and hid the interior.

Billy rose and walked boldly inside. If he could see no one within, then no one could see him once he was inside the door. Therefore, so reasoned Billy Byrne, he would have as good a chance as the occupants of the hut, should they prove to be enemies.

He crossed the floor carefully, stopping often to listen. At last he heard a rustling sound just ahead of him. His fingers tightened upon the revolver he carried in his right hand, by the barrel, clublike. Billy had no intention of making any more noise than necessary.

Again he heard a sound from the same direction. It was not at all unlike the frightened gasp of a woman. Billy emitted a low growl, in fair imitation of a prowling dog that has been disturbed.

Again the gasp, and a low: "Go away!" in liquid feminine tones — and in English!

Billy uttered a low: "S-s-sh!" and tiptoed closer. Extending his hands they presently came in contact with a human body which shrank from him with another smothered cry.

"Barbara!" whispered Billy, bending closer.

A hand reached out through the darkness, found him, and closed upon his sleeve.

"Who are you?" asked a low voice.

"Billy," he replied. "Are you alone in here?"

"No, an old woman guards me," replied the girl, and at the same time they both heard a movement close at hand, and something scurried past them to be silhouetted for an instant against the path of lesser darkness which marked the location of the doorway.

"There she goes!" cried Barbara. "She heard you and she has gone for help."

"Then come!" said Billy, seizing the girl's arm and dragging her to her feet; but they had scarce crossed half the distance to the doorway when the cries of the old woman without warned them that the camp was being aroused.

Billy thrust a revolver into Barbara's hand. "We gotta

make a fight of it, little girl," he said. "But you'd better die than be here alone."

As they emerged from the hut they saw warriors running from every doorway. The old woman stood screaming in Piman at the top of her lungs. Billy, keeping Barbara in front of him that he might shield her body with his own, turned directly out of the village. He did not fire at first hoping that they might elude detection and thus not draw the fire of the Indians upon them; but he was doomed to disappointment, and they had taken scarcely a dozen steps when a rifle spoke above the noise of human voices and a bullet whizzed past them.

Then Billy replied, and Barbara, too, from just behind his shoulder. Together they backed away toward the shadow of the trees beyond the village and as they went they poured shot after shot into the village.

The Indians, but just awakened and still half stupid from sleep, did not know but that they were attacked by a vastly superior force, and this fear held them in check for several minutes — long enough for Billy and Barbara to reach the summit of the bluff from which Billy and Eddie had first been fired upon.

Here they were hidden from the view of the Indians, and Billy broke at once into a run, half carrying the girl with a strong arm about her waist.

"If we can reach the foothills," he said, "I think we can dodge 'em, an' by goin' all night we may reach the river and El Orobo by morning. It's a long hike, Barbara, but we gotta make it — we gotta, for if daylight finds us in the Piman country we won't never make it. Anyway," he concluded optimistically, "it's all down hill."

"We'll make it, Billy," she replied, "if we can get past the sentry."

"What sentry?" asked Billy. "I didn't see no sentry

when I come in."

"They keep a sentry way down the trail all night," replied the girl. "In the daytime he is nearer the village — on the top of this bluff, for from here he can see the whole valley; but at night they station him farther away in a narrow part of the trail."

"It's a mighty good thing you tipped me off," said Billy; "for I'd a-run right into him. I thought they was all behind us now."

After that they went more cautiously, and when they reached the part of the trail where the sentry might be expected to be found, Barbara warned Billy of the fact. Like two thieves they crept along in the shadow of the canyon wall. Inwardly Billy cursed the darkness of the night which hid from view everything more than a few paces from them; yet it may have been this very darkness which saved them, since it hid them as effectually from an enemy as it hid the enemy from them. They had reached the point where Barbara was positive the sentry should be. The girl was clinging tightly to Billy's left arm. He could feel the pressure of her fingers as they sunk into his muscles, sending little tremors and thrills through his giant frame. Even in the face of death Billy Byrne could sense the ecstasies of personal contact with this girl — the only woman he ever had loved or ever would.

And then a black shadow loomed before them, and a rifle flashed in their faces without a word or a sign of warning.

Chapter XVII

"YOU ARE MY GIRL!"

Mr. Anthony Harding was pacing back and forth the length of the veranda of the ranchhouse at El Orobo waiting for some word of hope from those who had ridden out in search of his daughter, Barbara. Each swirling dust devil that eddied across the dry flat on either side of the river roused hopes within his breast that it might have been spurred into activity by the hoofs of a pony bearing a messenger of good tidings; but always his hopes were dashed, for no horseman emerged from the heat haze of the distance where the little dust devils raced playfully among the cacti and the greasewood.

But at last, in the northwest, a horseman, unheralded by gyrating dust column, came into sight. Mr. Harding shook his head sorrowfully. It had not been from this direction that he had expected word of Barbara, yet he kept his eyes fastened upon the rider until the latter reined in at the ranchyard and loped a tired and sweating pony to the foot of the veranda steps. Then Mr.

Harding saw who the newcomer was.

"Bridge!" he exclaimed. "What brings you back here? Don't you know that you endanger us as well as yourself by being seen here? General Villa will think that we have been harboring you."

Bridge swung from the saddle and ran up onto the veranda. He paid not the slightest attention to Anthony Harding's protest.

"How many men you got here that you can depend on?" he asked.

"None," replied the Easterner. "What do you mean?"

"None!" cried Bridge, incredulity and hopelessness showing upon his countenance. "Isn't there a Chinaman and a couple of faithful Mexicans?"

"Oh, yes, of course," assented Mr. Harding; "but what are you driving at?"

"Pesita is on his way here to clean up El Orobo. He can't be very far behind me. Call the men you got, and we'll get together all the guns and ammunition on the ranch, and barricade the ranchhouse. We may be able to stand 'em off. Have you heard anything of Miss Barbara?"

Anthony Harding shook his head sadly.

"Then we'll have to stay right here and do the best we can," said Bridge. "I was thinking we might make a run for it if Miss Barbara was here; but as she's not we must wait for those who went out after her."

Mr. Harding summoned the two Mexicans while Bridge ran to the cookhouse and ordered the Chinaman to the ranchhouse. Then the erstwhile bookkeeper ransacked the bunkhouse for arms and ammunition. What little he found he carried to the ranchhouse, and with the help of the others barricaded the doors and windows of the first floor.

"We'll have to make our fight from the upper windows," he explained to the ranch owner. "If Pesita doesn't bring too large a force we may be able to stand them off until you can get help from Cuivaca. Call up there now and see if you can get Villa to send help — he ought to protect you from Pesita. I understand that there is no love lost between the two."

Anthony Harding went at once to the telephone and rang for the central at Cuivaca.

"Tell it to the operator," shouted Bridge who stood peering through an opening in the barricade before a front window; "they are coming now, and the chances are that the first thing they'll do is cut the telephone wires."

The Easterner poured his story and appeal for help into the ears of the girl at the other end of the line, and then for a few moments there was silence in the room as he listened to her reply.

"Impossible!" and "My God! it can't be true," Bridge heard the older man ejaculate, and then he saw him hang up the receiver and turn from the instrument, his face drawn and pinched with an expression of utter hopelessness.

"What's wrong?" asked Bridge.

"Villa has turned against the Americans," replied Harding, dully. The operator evidently feels friendly toward us, for she warned me not to appeal to Villa and told me why. Even now, this minute, the man has a force of twenty-five hundred ready to march on Columbus, New Mexico. Three Americans were hanged in Cuivaca this afternoon. It's horrible, sir! It's horrible! We are as good as dead this very minute. Even if we stand off Pesita we can never escape to the border through Villa's forces."

"It looks bad," admitted Bridge. "In fact it couldn't look much worse; but here we are, and while our ammunition holds out about all we can do is stay here and use it. Will you men stand by us?" he addressed the Chinaman and the two Mexicans, who assured him that they had no love for Pesita and would fight for Anthony Harding in preference to going over to the enemy.

"Good!" exclaimed Bridge, "and now for upstairs. They'll be howling around here in about five minutes, and we want to give them a reception they won't forget."

He led the way to the second floor, where the five took up positions near the front windows. A short distance from the ranchhouse they could see the enemy, consisting of a detachment of some twenty of Pesita's troopers riding at a brisk trot in their direction.

"Pesita's with them," announced Bridge, presently. "He's the little fellow on the sorrel. Wait until they are close up, then give them a few rounds; but go easy on the ammunition — we haven't any too much."

Pesita, expecting no resistance, rode boldly into the ranchyard. At the bunkhouse and the office his little force halted while three or four troopers dismounted and entered the buildings in search of victims. Disappointed there they moved toward the ranchhouse.

"Lie low!" Bridge cautioned his companions. "Don't let them see you, and wait till I give the word before you fire."

On came the horsemen at a slow walk. Bridge waited until they were within a few yards of the house, then he cried: "Now! Let 'em have it!" A rattle of rifle fire broke from the upper windows into the ranks of the Pesitistas. Three troopers reeled and slipped from their saddles. Two horses dropped in their tracks. Cursing and yelling, the balance of the horsemen wheeled and galloped away in the direction of the office building, followed by the fire of the defenders.

"That wasn't so bad," cried Bridge. "I'll venture a guess that Mr. Pesita is some surprised — and sore.

There they go behind the office. They'll stay there a few minutes talking it over and getting up their courage to try it again. Next time they'll come from another direction. You two," he continued, turning to the Mexicans, "take positions on the east and south sides of the house. Sing can remain here with Mr. Harding. I'll take the north side facing the office. Shoot at the first man who shows his head. If we can hold them off until dark we may be able to get away. Whatever happens don't let one of them get close enough to fire the house. That's what they'll try for."

It was fifteen minutes before the second attack came. Five dismounted troopers made a dash for the north side of the house; but when Bridge dropped the first of them before he had taken ten steps from the office building and wounded a second the others retreated for shelter.

Time and again as the afternoon wore away Pesita made attempts to get men close up to the house; but in each instance they were driven back, until at last they desisted from their efforts to fire the house or rush it, and contented themselves with firing an occasional shot through the windows opposite them.

"They're waiting for dark," said Bridge to Mr. Harding during a temporary lull in the hostilities, "and then we're goners, unless the boys come back from across the river in time."

"Couldn't we get away after dark?" asked the Easterner.

"It's our only hope if help don't reach us," replied Bridge.

But when night finally fell and the five men made an attempt to leave the house upon the side away from the office building they were met with the flash of carbines and the ping of bullets. One of the Mexican defenders fell, mortally wounded, and the others were barely able to drag him within and replace the barricade before the door when five of Pesita's men charged close up to their defenses. These were finally driven off and again there came a lull; but all hope of escape was gone, and Bridge reposted the defenders at the upper windows where they might watch every approach to the house.

As the hours dragged on the hopelessness of their position grew upon the minds of all. Their ammunition was almost gone — each man had but a few rounds remaining — and it was evident that Pesita, through an inordinate desire for revenge, would persist until he had reduced their fortress and claimed the last of them as his victim.

It was with such cheerful expectations that they awaited the final assault which would see them without ammunition and defenseless in the face of a cruel and implacable foe.

It was just before daylight that the anticipated rush occurred. From every side rang the reports of carbines and the yells of the bandits. There were scarcely more than a dozen of the original twenty left; but they made up for their depleted numbers by the rapidity with which they worked their firearms and the loudness and ferocity of their savage cries.

And this time they reached the shelter of the veranda and commenced battering at the door.

At the report of the rifle so close to them Billy Byrne shoved Barbara quickly to one side and leaped forward to close with the man who barred their way to liberty.

That they had surprised him even more than he had them was evidenced by the wildness of his shot which passed harmlessly above their heads as well as by the fact that he had permitted them to come so close before engaging them.

To the latter event was attributable his undoing, for

it permitted Billy Byrne to close with him before the
Indian could reload his antiquated weapon. Down the
two men went, the American on top, each striving for
a deathhold; but in weight and strength and skill the
Piman was far outclassed by the trained fighter, a part
of whose daily workouts had consisted in wrestling
with proficient artists of the mat.

Barbara Harding ran forward to assist her champion
but as the men rolled and tumbled over the ground
she could find no opening for a blow that might not
endanger Billy Byrne quite as much as it endangered
his antagonist; but presently she discovered that the
American required no assistance. She saw the Indian's
head bending slowly forward beneath the resistless
force of the other's huge muscles, she heard the crack
that announced the parting of the vertebrae and saw
the limp thing which had but a moment before been
a man, pulsing with life and vigor, roll helplessly aside
— a harmless and inanimate lump of clay.

Billy Byrne leaped to his feet, shaking himself as a
great mastiff might whose coat had been ruffled in a
fight.

"Come!" he whispered. "We gotta beat it now for
sure. That guy's shot'll lead 'em right down to us," and
once more they took up their flight down toward the
valley, along an unknown trail through the darkness
of the night.

For the most part they moved in silence, Billy holding the girl's arm or hand to steady her over the rough
and dangerous portions of the path. And as they went
there grew in Billy's breast a love so deep and so
resistless that he found himself wondering that he had
ever imagined that his former passion for this girl was
love.

This new thing surged through him and over him
with all the blind, brutal, compelling force of a mighty

tidal wave. It battered down and swept away the frail barriers of his new-found gentleness. Again he was the Mucker — hating the artificial wall of social caste which separated him from this girl; but now he was ready to climb the wall, or, better still, to batter it down with his huge fists. But the time was not yet — first he must get Barbara to a place of safety.

On and on they went. The night grew cold. Far ahead there sounded the occasional pop of a rifle. Billy wondered what it could mean and as they approached the ranch and he discovered that it came from that direction he hastened their steps to even greater speed than before.

"Somebody's shootin' up the ranch," he volunteered. "Wonder who it could be."

"Suppose it is your friend and general?" asked the girl.

Billy made no reply. They reached the river and as Billy knew not where the fords lay he plunged in at the point at which the water first barred their progress and dragging the girl after him, plowed bull-like for the opposite shore. Where the water was above his depth he swam while Barbara clung to his shoulders. Thus they made the passage quickly and safely.

Billy stopped long enough to shake the water out of his carbine, which the girl had carried across, and then forged ahead toward the ranchhouse from which the sounds of battle came now in increased volume.

And at the ranchhouse "hell was popping." The moment Bridge realized that some of the attackers had reached the veranda he called the surviving Mexican and the Chinaman to follow him to the lower floor where they might stand a better chance to repel this new attack. Mr. Harding he persuaded to remain upstairs.

Outside a dozen men were battering to force an

entrance. Already one panel had splintered, and as Bridge entered the room he could see the figures of the bandits through the hole they had made. Raising his rifle he fired through the aperture. There was a scream as one of the attackers dropped; but the others only increased their efforts, their oaths, and their threats of vengeance.

The three defenders poured a few rounds through the sagging door, then Bridge noted that the Chinaman ceased firing.

"What's the matter?" he asked.

"Allee gonee," replied Sing, pointing to his ammunition belt.

At the same instant the Mexican threw down his carbine and rushed for a window on the opposite side of the room. His ammunition was exhausted and with it had departed his courage. Flight seemed the only course remaining. Bridge made no effort to stop him. He would have been glad to fly, too; but he could not leave Anthony Harding, and he was sure that the older man would prove unequal to any sustained flight on foot.

"You better go, too, Sing," he said to the Chinaman, placing another bullet through the door; "there's nothing more that you can do, and it may be that they are all on this side now — I think they are. You fellows have fought splendidly. Wish I could give you something more substantial than thanks; but that's all I have now and shortly Pesita won't even leave me that much."

"Allee light," replied Sing cheerfully, and a second later he was clambering through the window in the wake of the loyal Mexican.

And then the door crashed in and half a dozen troopers followed by Pesita himself burst into the room.

Bridge was standing at the foot of the stairs, his

carbine clubbed, for he had just spent his last bullet. He knew that he must die; but he was determined to make them purchase his life as dearly as he could, and to die in defense of Anthony Harding, the father of the girl he loved, even though hopelessly.

Pesita saw from the American's attitude that he had no more ammunition. He struck up the carbine of a trooper who was about to shoot Bridge down.

"Wait!" commanded the bandit. "Cease firing! His ammunition is gone. Will you surrender?" he asked of Bridge.

"Not until I have beaten from the heads of one or two of your friends," he replied, "that which their egotism leads them to imagine are brains. No, if you take me alive, Pesita, you will have to kill me to do it."

Pesita shrugged. "Very well," he said, indifferently, "it makes little difference to me — that stairway is as good as a wall. These brave defenders of the liberty of poor, bleeding Mexico will make an excellent firing squad. Attention, my children! Ready! Aim!"

Eleven carbines were leveled at Bridge. In the ghastly light of early dawn the sallow complexions of the Mexicans took on a weird hue. The American made a wry face, a slight shudder shook his slender frame, and then he squared his shoulders and looked Pesita smilingly in the face,

The figure of a man appeared at the window through which the Chinaman and the loyal Mexican had escaped. Quick eyes took in the scene within the room.

"Hey!" he yelled. "Cut the rough stuff!" and leaped into the room.

Pesita, surprised by the interruption, turned toward the intruder before he had given the command to fire. A smile lit his features when he saw who it was.

"Ah!" he exclaimed, "my dear Captain Byrne. Just in time to see a traitor and a spy pay the penalty for his crimes."

"Nothin' doin'," growled Billy Byrne, and then he threw his carbine to his shoulder and took careful aim at Pesita's face.

How easy it would have been to have hesitated a moment in the window before he made his presence known — just long enough for Pesita to speak the single word that would have sent eleven bullets speeding into the body of the man who loved Barbara and whom Billy believed the girl loved. But did such a thought occur to Billy Byrne of Grand Avenue? It did not. He forgot every other consideration beyond his loyalty to a friend. Bridge and Pesita were looking at him in wide-eyed astonishment.

"Lay down your carbines!" Billy shot his command at the firing squad. "Lay 'em down or I'll bore Pesita. Tell 'em to lay 'em down, Pesita. I gotta bead on your beezer."

Pesita did as he was bid, his yellow face pasty with rage.

"Now their cartridge belts!" snapped Billy, and when these had been deposited upon the floor he told Bridge to disarm the bandit chief.

"Is Mr. Harding safe?" he asked of Bridge, and receiving an affirmative he called upstairs for the older man to descend.

As Mr. Harding reached the foot of the stairs Barbara entered the room by the window through which Billy had come — a window which opened upon the side veranda.

"Now we gotta hike," announced Billy. "It won't never be safe for none of you here after this, not even if you do think Villa's your friend — which he ain't the friend of no American."

"We know that now," said Mr. Harding, and repeated to Billy that which the telephone operator had told him earlier in the day.

Marching Pesita and his men ahead of them Billy and the others made their way to the rear of the office building where the horses of the bandits were tethered. They were each armed now from the discarded weapons of the raiders, and well supplied with ammunition. The Chinaman and the loyal Mexican also discovered themselves when they learned that the tables had been turned upon Pesita. They, too, were armed and all were mounted, and when Billy had loaded the remaining weapons upon the balance of the horses the party rode away, driving Pesita's live stock and arms ahead of them.

"I imagine," remarked Bridge, "that you've rather discouraged pursuit for a while at least," but pursuit came sooner than they had anticipated.

They had reached a point on the river not far from Jose's when a band of horsemen appeared approaching from the west. Billy urged his party to greater speed that they might avoid a meeting if possible; but it soon became evident that the strangers had no intention of permitting them to go unchallenged, for they altered their course and increased their speed so that they were soon bearing down upon the fugitives at a rapid gallop.

"I guess," said Billy, "that we'd better open up on 'em. It's a cinch they ain't no friends of ours anywhere in these parts."

"Hadn't we better wait a moment," said Mr. Harding; "we do not want to chance making any mistake."

"It ain't never a mistake to shoot a Dago," replied Billy. His eyes were fastened upon the approaching horsemen, and he presently gave an exclamation of recognition. "There's Rozales," he said. "I couldn't mistake that beanpole nowheres. We're safe enough in takin' a shot at 'em if Rosie's with 'em. He's Pesita's head guy," and he drew his revolver and took a single shot in the direction of his former comrades. Bridge followed his example. The oncoming Pesitistas reined in. Billy returned his revolver to its holster and drew his carbine.

"You ride on ahead," he said to Mr. Harding and Barbara. "Bridge and I'll bring up the rear."

Then he stopped his pony and turning took deliberate aim at the knot of horsemen to their left. A bandit tumbled from his saddle and the fight was on.

Fortunately for the Americans Rozales had but a handful of men with him and Rozales himself was never keen for a fight in the open.

All morning he hovered around the rear of the escaping Americans; but neither side did much damage to the other, and during the afternoon Billy noticed that Rozales merely followed within sight of them, after having dispatched one of his men back in the direction from which they had come.

"After reinforcements," commented Byrne.

All day they rode without meeting with any roving bands of soldiers or bandits, and the explanation was all too sinister to the Americans when coupled with the knowledge that Villa was to attack an American town that night.

"I wish we could reach the border in time to warn 'em," said Billy; "but they ain't no chance. If we cross before sunup tomorrow morning we'll be doin' well."

He had scarcely spoken to Barbara Harding all day, for his duties as rear guard had kept him busy; nor had he conversed much with Bridge, though he had often eyed the latter whose gaze wandered many times to the slender, graceful figure of the girl ahead of them.

Billy was thinking as he never had thought before. It seemed to him a cruel fate that had so shaped their destinies that his best friend loved the girl Billy loved. That Bridge was ignorant of Billy's infatuation for her the latter well knew. He could not blame Bridge, nor could he, upon the other hand, quite reconcile himself to the more than apparent adoration which marked his friend's attitude toward Barbara.

As daylight waned the fugitives realized from the shuffling gait of their mounts, from drooping heads and dull eyes that rest was imperative. They themselves were fagged, too, and when a ranchhouse loomed in front of them they decided to halt for much-needed recuperation.

Here they found three Americans who were totally unaware of Villa's contemplated raid across the border, and who when they were informed of it were doubly glad to welcome six extra carbines, for Barbara not only was armed but was eminently qualified to expend ammunition without wasting it.

Rozales and his small band halted out of range of the ranch; but they went hungry while their quarry fed themselves and their tired mounts.

The Clark brothers and their cousin, a man by the name of Mason, who were the sole inhabitants of the ranch counseled a long rest — two hours at least, for the border was still ten miles away and speed at the last moment might be their sole means of salvation.

Billy was for moving on at once before the reinforcements, for which he was sure Rozales had dispatched his messenger, could overtake them. But the others were tired and argued, too, that upon jaded ponies they could not hope to escape and so they waited, until, just as they were ready to continue their flight, flight became impossible.

Darkness had fallen when the little party commenced to resaddle their ponies and in the midst of their labors there came a rude and disheartening interruption. Billy had kept either the Chinaman or Bridge constantly upon watch toward the direction in which

Rozales' men lolled smoking in the dark, and it was the crack of Bridge's carbine which awoke the Americans to the fact that though the border lay but a few miles away they were still far from safety.

As he fired Bridge turned in his saddle and shouted to the others to make for the shelter of the ranchhouse.

"There are two hundred of them," he cried. "Run for cover!"

Billy and the Clark brothers leaped to their saddles and spurred toward the point where Bridge sat pumping lead into the advancing enemy. Mason and Mr. Harding hurried Barbara to the questionable safety of the ranchhouse. The Mexican followed them, and Bridge ordered Sing back to assist in barricading the doors and windows, while he and Billy and the Clark boys held the bandits in momentary check.

Falling back slowly and firing constantly as they came the four approached the house while Pesita and his full band advanced cautiously after them. They had almost reached the house when Bridge lunged forward from his saddle. The Clark boys had dismounted and were leading their ponies inside the house. Billy alone noted the wounding of his friend. Without an instant's hesitation he slipped from his saddle, ran back to where Bridge lay and lifted him in his arms. Bullets were pattering thick about them. A horseman far in advance of his fellows galloped forward with drawn saber to cut down the gringos.

Billy, casting an occasional glance behind, saw the danger in time to meet it — just, in fact, as the weapon was cutting through the air toward his head. Dropping Bridge and dodging to one side he managed to escape the cut, and before the swordsman could recover Billy had leaped to his pony's side and seizing the rider about the waist dragged him to the ground.

"Rozales!" he exclaimed, and struck the man as he

had never struck another in all his life, with the full force of his mighty muscles backed by his great weight, with clenched fist full in the face.

There was a spurting of blood and a splintering of bone, and Captain Guillermo Rozales sank senseless to the ground, his career of crime and rapine ended forever.

Again Billy lifted Bridge in his arms and this time he succeeded in reaching the ranchhouse without opposition though a little crimson stream trickled down his left arm to drop upon the face of his friend as he deposited Bridge upon the floor of the house.

All night the Pesitistas circled the lone ranchhouse. All night they poured their volleys into the adobe walls and through the barricaded windows. All night the little band of defenders fought gallantly for their lives; but as day approached the futility of their endeavors was borne in upon them, for of the nine one was dead and three wounded, and the numbers of their assailants seemed undiminished.

Billy Byrne had been lying all night upon his stomach before a window firing out into the darkness at the dim forms which occasionally showed against the dull, dead background of the moonless desert.

Presently he leaped to his feet and crossed the floor to the room in which the horses had been placed.

"Everybody fire toward the rear of the house as fast as they can," said Billy. "I want a clear space for my getaway."

"Where you goin?" asked one of the Clark brothers.

"North," replied Billy, "after some of Funston's men on the border."

"But they won't cross," said Mr. Harding. "Washington won't let them."

"They gotta," snapped Billy Byrne, "an' they will when they know there's an American girl here with a bunch of Dagos yappin' around."

"You'll be killed," said Price Clark. "You can't never get through."

"Leave it to me," replied Billy. "Just get ready an' open that back door when I give the word, an' then shut it again in a hurry when I've gone through."

He led a horse from the side room, and mounted it.

"Open her up, boes!" he shouted, and "S'long everybody!"

Price Clark swung the door open. Billy put spurs to his mount and threw himself forward flat against the animal's neck. Another moment he was through and a rattling fusillade of shots proclaimed the fact that his bold feat had not gone unnoted by the foe.

The little Mexican pony shot like a bolt from a crossbow out across the level desert. The rattling of carbines only served to add speed to its frightened feet. Billy sat erect in the saddle, guiding the horse with his left hand and working his revolver methodically with his right.

At a window behind him Barbara Harding stood breathless and spellbound until he had disappeared into the gloom of the early morning darkness to the north, then she turned with a weary sigh and resumed her place beside the wounded Bridge whose head she bathed with cool water, while he tossed in the delirium of fever.

The first streaks of daylight were piercing the heavens, the Pesitistas were rallying for a decisive charge, the hopes of the little band of besieged were at low ebb when from the west there sounded the pounding of many hoofs.

"Villa," moaned Westcott Clark, hopelessly. "We're done for now, sure enough. He must be comin' back from his raid on the border."

In the faint light of dawn they saw a column of

horsemen deploy suddenly into a long, thin line which galloped forward over the flat earth, coming toward them like a huge, relentless engine of destruction.

The Pesitistas were watching too. They had ceased firing and sat in their saddles forgetful of their contemplated charge.

The occupants of the ranchhouse were gathered at the small windows.

"What's them?" cried Mason — "them things floating over 'em."

"They're guidons!" exclaimed Price Clark "— the guidons of the United States cavalry regiment. See 'em! See 'em? God! but don't they look good?"

There was a wild whoop from the lungs of the advancing cavalrymen. Pesita's troops answered it with a scattering volley, and a moment later the Americans were among them in that famous revolver charge which is now history.

Daylight had come revealing to the watchers in the ranchhouse the figures of the combatants. In the thick of the fight loomed the giant figure of a man in nondescript garb which more closely resembled the apparel of the Pesitistas than it did the uniforms of the American soldiery, yet it was with them he fought. Barbara's eyes were the first to detect him.

"There's Mr. Byrne," she cried. "It must have been he who brought the troops."

"Why, he hasn't had time to reach the border yet," remonstrated one of the Clark boys, "much less get back here with help."

"There he is though," said Mr. Harding. "It's certainly strange. I can't understand what American troops are doing across the border — especially under the present administration."

The Pesitistas held their ground for but a moment then they wheeled and fled; but not before Pesita himself had forced his pony close to that of Billy Byrne.

"Traitor!" screamed the bandit. "You shall die for this," and fired point-blank at the American.

Billy felt a burning sensation in his already wounded left arm; but his right was still good.

"For poor, bleeding Mexico!" he cried, and put a bullet through Pesita's forehead.

*U*nder escort of the men of the Thirteenth Cavalry who had pursued Villa's raiders into Mexico and upon whom Billy Byrne had stumbled by chance, the little party of fugitives came safely to United States soil, where all but one breathed sighs of heartfelt relief.

Bridge was given first aid by members of the hospital corps, who assured Billy that his friend would not die. Mr. Harding and Barbara were taken in by the wife of an officer, and it was at the quarters of the latter that Billy Byrne found her alone in the sitting-room.

The girl looked up as he entered, a sad smile upon her face. She was about to ask him of his wound; but he gave her no opportunity.

"I've come for you," he said. "I gave you up once when I thought it was better for you to marry a man in your own class. I won't give you up again. You're mine — you're my girl, and I'm goin' to take you with me. Were goin' to Galveston as fast as we can, and from there we're goin' to Rio. You belonged to me long before Bridge saw you. He can't have you. Nobody can have you but me, and if anyone tries to keep me from taking you they'll get killed."

He took a step nearer that brought him close to her. She did not shrink — only looked up into his face with wide eyes filled with wonder. He seized her roughly in his arms.

"You are my girl!" he cried hoarsely. "Kiss me!"

"Wait!" she said. "First tell me what you meant by saying that Bridge couldn't have me. I never knew that Bridge wanted me, and I certainly have never wanted Bridge. O Billy! Why didn't you do this long ago? Months ago in New York I wanted you to take me; but you left me to another man whom I didn't love. I thought you had ceased to care, Billy, and since we have been together here — since that night in the room back of the office — you have made me feel that I was nothing to you. Take me, Billy! Take me anywhere in the world that you go. I love you and I'll slave for you — anything just to be with you."

"Barbara!" cried Billy Byrne, and then his voice was smothered by the pressure of warm, red lips against his own.

A half hour later Billy stepped out into the street to make his way to the railroad station that he might procure transportation for three to Galveston. Anthony Harding was going with them. He had listened to Barbara's pleas, and had finally volunteered to back Billy Byrne's flight from the jurisdiction of the law, or at least to a place where, under a new name, he could start life over again and live it as the son-in-law of old Anthony Harding should live.

Among the crowd viewing the havoc wrought by the raiders the previous night was a large man with a red face. It happened that he turned suddenly about as Billy Byrne was on the point of passing behind him. Both men started as recognition lighted their faces and he of the red face found himself looking down the barrel of a six-shooter.

"Put it up, Byrne," he admonished the other coolly. "I didn't know you were so good on the draw."

"I'm good on the draw all right, Flannagan," said

Billy, "and I ain't drawin' for amusement neither. I gotta chance to get away and live straight, and have a little happiness in life, and, Flannagan, the man who tries to crab my game is goin' to get himself croaked. I'll never go back to stir alive. See?"

"Yep," said Flannagan, "I see; but I ain't tryin' to crab your game. I ain't down here after you this trip. Where you been, anyway, that you don't know the war's over? Why Coke Sheehan confessed a month ago that it was him that croaked Schneider, and the governor pardoned you about ten days ago."

"You stringin' me?" asked Billy, a vicious glint in his eyes.

"On the level," Flannagan assured him. "Wait, I gotta clippin' from the Trib in my clothes somewheres that gives all the dope."

He drew some papers from his coat pocket and handed one to Billy.

"Turn your back and hold up your hands while I read," said Byrne, and as Flannagan did as he was bid Billy unfolded the soiled bit of newspaper and read that which set him a-trembling with nervous excitement.

A moment later Detective Sergeant Flannagan ventured a rearward glance to note how Byrne was receiving the joyful tidings which the newspaper article contained.

"Well, I'll be!" ejaculated the sleuth, for Billy Byrne was already a hundred yards away and breaking all records in his dash for the sitting-room he had quitted but a few minutes before.

It was a happy and contented trio who took the train the following day on their way back to New York City after bidding Bridge good-bye in the improvised hospital and exacting his promise that he would visit them in New York in the near future.

*I*t was a month later; spring was filling the southland with new, sweet life. The joy of living was reflected in the song of birds and the opening of buds. Beside a slow-moving stream a man squatted before a tiny fire. A battered tin can, half filled with water stood close to the burning embers. Upon a sharpened stick the man roasted a bit of meat, and as he watched it curling at the edges as the flame licked it he spoke aloud though there was none to hear:

> Just for a con I'd like to know (yes, he crossed
>   over long ago;
> And he was right, believe me, bo!) if somewhere in
>   the South,
> Down where the clouds lie on the sea, he found
>   his sweet Penelope
> With buds of roses in her hair and kisses on her
>   mouth.

"Which is what they will be singing about me one of these days," he commented.

CPSIA information can be obtained at www.ICGtesting.com
Printed in the USA
266587BV00002B/50/A